# DEAD LOVE

## LINDA WELLS

# DEAD LOVE

## by

## Linda Wells

This book is a work of fiction. Names, characters, organizations, institutions, businesses, locales, and events are the product of the author's imagination or are used fictitiously. All characters appearing in this work are entirely the work of the author's imagination and any resemblance to actual persons, living or dead, is purely coincidental.

ISBN-10: 1480262072
ISBN-13: 9781480262072

Library of Congress Control Number: 2012921178

CreateSpace Independent Publishing Platform
North Charleston, South Carolina

# I

Maggie Ryan was running late. Her alarm hadn't gone off, so she had rushed through the shower, leaving Mike in bed to catch a few extra minutes of sleep. He would have to deal with getting the boys to school. He worked at home, and his schedule was flexible. Since Pembrooke Academy was only a few blocks away, he could walk them to school. He enjoyed grabbing a cappuccino and bagel at the local coffee shop on his way home.

After her shower, Maggie dressed in beige string bikini panties, matching lacey bra, sheer stockings, and a straight "just above the knee" taupe skirt, crisp white tailored blouse, and a classic fitted navy blazer with gold buttons. She slipped on her taupe heels and then stood in front of the full-length mirror to see if the gold wings on her left lapel were straight. After brushing her long blonde hair, Maggie pulled it back in a sleek ponytail, fastened with a tortoise shell clasp. The look was chic and professional. She applied light powder, smoky brown eye shadow and liner, mascara, blush, and a neutral pink lipstick. She was a natural beauty with full lips and light blue eyes, the makeup adding the finishing touch. Maggie was a flight attendant for Century Air, a "senior stew," with ten years of service. She was flying a turnaround to Miami out of LaGuardia three days a week. The days were long, ten hours plus, but the work was exciting. In spite of the inevitable flight delays and the occasional irritable passenger, the job was fun and each day was different. In addition, she liked the perks. She and Mike loved to travel, and the job offered them that opportunity.

Maggie gulped down the last of her coffee, took the cup into the kitchen, and slipped into the bedroom to say good-bye to Mike. She leaned over the bed where he was deep in sleep, whispering, "Wake up, Mike. It's time to get the boys ready for school."

He yawned and said, "Good morning, lover," in his sleepy, sexy voice.

He put his arms around her hips and tried to pull her into bed with him. He was boyishly handsome, with long sandy brown hair, which fell over his forehead, blue eyes, and subtly rugged features. His rough beard was so masculine, and she loved feeling his face against hers when they kissed. His arms were still around her as her lips brushed his, and he responded, touching her leg, sliding his hand up her skirt, touching her silky panties.

She reluctantly pulled away from him, saying, "Later, sweetheart. I love you, but I have to go," while softly brushing his hair off his forehead with her fingertips.

Maggie rushed out of the bedroom. She would have loved to crawl into bed with him, memories of their passionate, earthy lovemaking from the night before still fresh in her mind, but she had to get to the airport. Thoughts of his body inside her made her ache for him, but she knew they would be together tonight. She couldn't wait to feel his arms around her as he held her close to him, naked, his body blended perfectly into hers. Their desire for each other was as intense as the day they met.

Though it was long commute to LaGuardia, they loved their West Side co-op. It was near the boys' school, Central Park, many great restaurants, shops, and historic sights. There was so much for them to enjoy by living in the city. Mike could work at home and take care of Mike Jr. and Tim when necessary. Besides writing for a scientific journal, Mike had published several books in his field of expertise, the biological and chemical sciences. They enjoyed city life, but escaped for occasional weekends to his family's cabin in the Poconos.

After a quick peek at the boys, still asleep, Maggie grabbed her small carry-on and purse and left the apartment. She caught the elevator to the lobby and hurried out of the building. She walked the short distance to the Express Subway Station entrance and took the stairs down to the dank platform. It was hot and muggy that early June Monday morning. She began to perspire but kept her pace. Checking her watch, she noted it was 6:45 a.m. She would have plenty of time to make the 7:30 a.m. check-in for the nine o'clock flight. She hated rushing, especially in this heat.

Maggie and the others on the congested platform felt harried and damp from the humidity. They grew impatient as they waited for the train. None had noticed the small gray aerosol canister sitting behind a cement support column in a dark recess of the station. The can was spraying quietly, releasing an odorless vapor straight up into the acrid, stagnant air. It was dispersing an invisible cloud, sending particles at least one hundred feet in all directions.

As the train came to a halt at the station, the automatic doors opened, and Maggie and the others pushed into the crowded car, everyone in a hurry to reach their destination.

# 2

It was early Monday morning and very busy in the emergency room at All Saints Hospital in downtown Manhattan. Several of the examination cubicles were occupied with critical patients from the night before, waiting for admission. Others had crying babies, children with the flu, or patients with open cuts that needed stitching. Several patients that had arrived with chest pain or abdominal pain had been examined, x-rayed, and needed further observation before being sent home. Dr. David Grant was a board-certified emergency room physician and director of the Emergency Department. His high standards and brusque manner kept the ER staff at peak performance. He would tolerate only the most skilled doctors and nurses. Some of the staff were afraid of him and his harsh criticism, but he was highly respected by all of his colleagues.

Dave was finally off duty after a twelve-hour shift. During those hours, Dr. Grant and the other two ER physicians and the nursing staff had seen eighty-four patients nonstop. He thrived on the adrenaline high of the job, but it was exhausting. He was in his office, located in the rear of the ER, behind the nurses' lounge. Sitting at his cluttered oak desk, reading glasses perched on the end of his nose, he studied the test results from one of the seriously ill patients remaining in the ER. Christina Noel, head nurse of the ER, had brought in the patient's chart and a cup of black coffee. She stood near him as he looked over the report.

Chris was staring at him as she waited for him to finish his thoughts. He had slate blue eyes, a graying crew cut and taut build. They shared the same passion and energy for their work and a deep mutual attraction. She placed the much needed coffee on his desk.

After studying the reports, Dave threw the papers on the desk, took his glasses off, and rubbed his eyes. He picked up the warm mug, took a sip, and said, "Thanks, Chris."

She asked, "How is he doing?"

Dr. Grant exhaled, leaning back in his chair, and replied, "He'll make it, but he needs a cardiologist. Call Dr. Stone and request a consult. He needs a cardiac cath and possible stent. I don't like the looks of his enzymes or his EKG."

Chris picked up the phone and called Dr. Stone's office, requesting the consult.

"She can see him this morning after finishing her rounds," said Chris.

"Good. Thanks, Chris." He looked up at her, realizing she had been watching at him.

Chris moved behind him and started rubbing his shoulders. She could feel him relax as she massaged his back and neck. She knew how exhausted he must be. It had been a tense night. When Dave started as the emergency room director, Chris was thrilled. She was thirty-five, divorced, and had found no man appealing until Dave. Everyone knew they were lovers, except his wife. Dave and Chris shared not only a drive for perfection but compassion for their patients. They made a great team, in and out of the hospital.

They had met a year ago when he moved from Vancouver, Washington, to Manhattan. He wanted the challenge of a New York hospital setting, where he was also on the teaching staff. It was a prestige position, and the money was excellent. His wife, Vicki, wasn't happy with the move and made that perfectly clear. Their twenty-year marriage was floundering anyway, but the move was the final blow. She had stayed with him, though, and moved to New York. The money, power, and status were all she wanted. Their unspoken agreement was that their marriage was one of convenience. She took care of his home and their teenage daughter, Carolyn, and portrayed the proper wife when he had to attend social functions. He gave her what she wanted, the large paycheck and, more importantly, the status of being married to a brilliant doctor. Image was everything to Vicki.

Chris was strikingly pretty, with shoulder-length auburn hair, deep brown eyes, and soft curves hidden under her scrubs. Dave turned his chair around and pulled her into his lap, kissing her mouth hard, as he slid his hand under her top. He unfastened her bra so he could feel her breasts. His fingers brushed her nipples, and the sensation made her wet. His hands on her full breasts made her nipples erect, and she uttered a low moan. He couldn't stop touching her, her breasts and every part of her. Her tongue in his mouth made him throb and he almost came when she unzipped his pants and began stroking him. They were still embraced as he pulled her toward the leather sofa. He stopped kissing her just long enough to pull her shoes, scrub bottoms, and panties off. His pants were still on when he started making love to her, sliding into her warm wetness. Their love for each other was so strong, and their sexual need was intense. They climaxed quickly; their orgasms seemed unending. It had been an exhausting night, but passion and love was their release for the stressful work they shared. They stayed wrapped together, holding each other close. Dave was still deep inside of her, whispering love words, never wanting to let go.

# 3

oey Caruso had to leave his small house in Queens at 5:30 a.m. His wife, Donna, had gotten up late, but managed to get his breakfast ready anyway. Her casual housekeeping sometimes irked him, but she was a loving wife and a good mother. Rosa was still sleeping in her crib when Joey quietly entered her room to see his baby girl in her pink sleeper, just for a moment. She was breathing softly, and he lovingly put his hand on her little body, just a warm touch to say good-bye for the day. She had just a shadow of fine dark brown hair and blue eyes. She had inherited his dark Italian coloring. He was still overwhelmed by the miracle God had given to him and Donna. Blowing her a small kiss, he crept from her room.

His breakfast was on the table. He was in his subway maintenance uniform, dark gray pants, and light gray shirt with his city badge, ID number and name on it. Joey yawned, tired from the weekend. He had stayed up too late watching the Yankees beat the White Sox. Though it was still early in the season, the Yankees showed great promise. Donna came over and kissed him on the lips. They gave each other a smile, and as she walked back to the sink, he gave her a gentle pat on her luscious behind. She and Rosa were his life, and he felt lucky as he looked around at the small kitchen and happy home they shared.

While eating, Joey asked, "Is my lunch made?"

She said, "Yes, and I put in your favorite dessert, too. A leftover slice of apple pie, a banana, plus the ham and cheese on rye that you like. Is that okay?"

He said, "Thanks, honey. I dread going to work today. It's going to be a hot one, and I am tired already."

"You should have come to bed early," Donna said, while giving him an enticing smile.

Joey said, "You're right. I'll make it up to you tonight."

Before leaving, he grabbed her and pulled her close for a special good-bye kiss. Now he really didn't want to leave. He would definitely go to bed early tonight, no matter what was on TV. Donna wanted another baby so Rosa could have a brother or sister, and besides that, he wanted to make love to his sexy wife.

They had met at a high school dance when Joey was a senior and Donna was only a sophomore. He had danced most of the night with Angela Martin, who had long legs and large breasts, along with a reputation for being easy. He kept noticing Donna standing with a few girlfriends and asked her to dance, a slow dance, and he loved the way she leaned against him and held him. The feel of her breath on his neck and her musky fragrance excited him. He kept pulling her closer to him and he could feel her respond. After their first dance, they were inseparable. Donna was wearing skin tight jeans and a low cut fluffy pink sweater that showed off her size C breasts, and Joey was captivated by this girl's sexy body. He wanted to feel her beautiful body against him, and not just when dancing.

One night in the back seat of his parents' car, they made love; it was the first for them both. It had been awkward and Joey was overwhelmed. He had to make love to this girl and make her his forever. He knew she was scared and so was he but she didn't say no to him and he knew she never would. He gave her his class ring that same night and told her he loved her and wanted to marry her. It was a promise he would keep.

Joey headed out the door to get to work by 6:15 a.m. It was a boring job, in some ways, but each day was different. He had many responsibilities, from maintenance and inspection of the subway platform, to cleaning the restrooms. He had not been able to get a better job with just two years at the community college. He and Donna were doing okay though, because she had worked in the makeup department at Macy's until Rosa came along. His city maintenance job for the Metropolitan Transit Authority paid well enough, and the benefits were great. A secure home and family meant a lot to Joey, but he often felt like a failure for not making more money and only being a glorified janitor. He knew Donna was proud of him no matter what he did. Their marriage wasn't perfect, but all in all, they had more than enough, and the love they shared was all the happiness she ever wanted. Baby Rosa had made their happiness complete.

# 4

D r. Suzy Chen left her condo at midnight and walked the five blocks, carrying only her purse and the package. The late model silver Taurus was just where they told her it would be.

The nondescript cutoff man was at the drop site at 3:00 a.m. The city was dark with few cars passing. Suzy Chen saw the shadowed figure standing at the bus stop. She pulled alongside the curb, lowered the passenger window, and the unknown contact strode forward, reaching into the window with gloved hand, grabbing the department store bag from the seat. Suzy clutched the .38 S&W with her left hand, invisible to the hooded figure.

He leaned forward and, in the briefest instant, with a raspy indistinguishable accent, asked, "How do I start the discharge?"

Suzy said, "There is a black lever, just under the lid of the canister. The lever beside the discharge valve… push it all the way to the right." She cautioned him. "Remember, it cannot be reversed, and the delay is only two minutes. Don't forget. Put the cap in this weighted bag and toss it in the river."

Those were the last words spoken. The contact turned so fast, she couldn't really see him, only his dark hooded sweatshirt, as he faded into the shadows.

Dr. Chen drove off slowly, careful to avoid notice. It took about three hours for her to get back to Edgewood. She left the car where she found it and walked quickly back to her condo. Her heart was beating rapidly. She was relieved to have gotten rid of the canister.

Chen was a respected biochemist and assistant director at Edgewood Laboratories, part of the Aberdeen Proving Grounds, and she had to be at work by eight o'clock. The return drive had given her time to decompress. She had labored for months, following with precision the instructions delivered to her by the Organization. The plan had been carefully formulated. Only two more tasks and her assignment would be complete.

The fear of discovery and the magnitude of the event overshadowed the exhilaration at what she had done. But the Director had assured her that she would be protected, and the rewards, on many levels, would be beyond gratifying.

What the Organization Director did not know was that her actions were also driven by a broken heart, which would directly avenge the man who had made many promises to her but had kept none.

# 5

It was in January that Suzy had met him at a dinner, hosted by the Secretary of the Army, at a luxury hotel in Baltimore, overlooking the Inner Harbor. Dr. Chen was in a high-profile position as assistant director of research and development at the Edgewood Laboratories. She was often a guest at formal governmental affairs. Beyond her status and accomplishment, she was a beautiful woman with striking Asian features, long straight black hair, and brown almond-shaped eyes of depth and eroticism. Her intellect, beauty, and reserved demeanor kept men from approaching. She was aloof and strictly professional at work, which heightened her sexual allure. Most of her staff were men, but all knew of her exacting work ethics and dared not cross any lines. She felt isolated, but that was part of the territory. Her level of concentration at work was intense, rendering her unable to be swayed by personal matters, but that did not keep her from being noticed and desired.

One of the service staff found her as she was going into the ladies' room, across the hall from the formal banquet room. He handed her a folded note. Suzy noted her name, handwritten in what appeared to be strong masculine script on the front. After thanking him, she entered the ladies' room, curious to know what the note contained.

Her eyes widened as she read the contents and absorbed the meaning. It was an invitation for cocktails in a private suite, here at the hotel, following the dinner. She ran a comb through her silky hair and added some gloss to her lips. She studied herself in the full-length mirror. Her red silk sheath, with mandarin collar, slit up the side, and black stiletto heels were perfect for this unexpected date. She was glad she had dressed in her sexiest red thong panties and bra to match her dress.

Suzy walked through the hotel lobby to the elevators, glad that the dinner had not lasted too long. She had sent the note back to him by one of the waiters, with only one word written on it: "Yes." She dated infrequently. Most men were hesitant to approach a woman of such mysterious beauty and intellect. Suzy was curious about this man who had attracted her gaze many times in the past. Now she knew he had noticed her as well.

She wasn't sure what to expect as she got off the elevator on the tenth floor and began walking down the formal carpeted hallway to his suite. He answered, dressed in dark slacks, white dress shirt, and dark gray tie, with his military tie bar as decoration. He was slightly taller than she, five feet nine inches, with muscular build, broad shoulders, and the confident demeanor of an experienced army officer. Lieutenant Colonel Maxwell Graham was well known for his military prowess and competence, not just for his past achievements, but in his current position as special service chief to the Joint Chiefs of Staff. His job was to assist in resolving matters that did not require JCS attention. He was based at Ft. Meade, but was often called to the Pentagon when needed for military updates and foreign policy meetings. He was an expert military strategist, having served in combat in some of the most dangerous special ops in Afghanistan and Iraq.

Colonel Graham warmly welcomed Dr. Chen. She followed him into the plush hotel suite and glanced around as they walked to the bar. The pale golden accents, beige carpet, yellow brocade sofa, and bronze sculpted lamps were elegant. The soft glow of lamplight muted the gold tones. The matching loveseat completed the setting, but her eyes were drawn to her host. This incredibly charming and powerful man intrigued her. His military bearing heightened his masculinity and strength and captivated her. She wondered how it would translate in the bedroom. She needed a man to be her intellectual and sexual equal.

Suzy had seen Max several times from a distance in professional settings. She found him interesting looking, but near him, she could get a better appreciation for his handsome face, strong chin, and penetrating blue eyes. He had brown hair with just a touch of gray and a sexy mouth. She had to maintain a cool detachment and catch her breath.

Graham asked, "Dr. Chen, what would you like to drink?"

She said, "Please call me Suzy, and Grand Marnier, if you have it."

He said, "Call me Max, and yes, I will have the same. It is my favorite aperitif."

After pouring their amber-colored drinks, he led her to the glass sliding doors that opened onto a balcony overlooking the Inner Harbor. The crisp, cool air smelled of the harbor, and the twinkling lights of the yachts reflecting off the water were beautiful.

Savoring her drink, "How lovely it is here," she observed, turning toward Max.

"Suzy, you are much lovelier, and thank you for joining me at the last minute. I have seen you several times at various meetings and at Aberdeen, but missed the chance to meet you. Your work is outstanding, from those I know at the APG. You are a biochemist?"

"Yes, Max."

The conversation flowed from there. He told her about his career history, where he had been stationed, and other details of his military life. He had attended the US Military Academy at West Point, as his father had, and become an army officer. He had achieved his goals and was committed to the values taught there—Duty, Honor, and Country. He had graduated as a second lieutenant and achieved greater responsibilities as he moved up in rank.

Suzy was fascinated and couldn't take her eyes off Max, preoccupied with feelings she couldn't describe. She didn't know if he felt the same distraction. He asked how she had chosen her field. Suzy began, saying her father was American and her mother Chinese and her parents had met when her father had traveled on business to Hong Kong. Her mother had taught music in Beijing before she was allowed to move to Hong Kong. Chinese society had allowed more freedoms then, and she was finally able to get a visa to come to the United States, where her parents were married. Her father was a chemistry professor at the University of Delaware, and Suzy, an only child, doted on by both parents, had learned ambition and hard work from them.

Max asked, "Why the Chinese last name?"

She said it was more of who she was and took her mother's maiden name as her own surname.

They were seeing only each other, as each word was spoken, and nothing else. Suzy was caught off guard when Max put his drink on the railing, and with his strong arms holding her so close against him, he looked down into her eyes. She felt herself melting into him. He gave her a soft kiss that became deep and wet. His body pushed against hers, and his tongue and mouth captured hers. Her fragrance was enticing, the scent pulling him to her, her body so desirable, he had to be closer to her. Her mouth responded, her body against his, and nothing else mattered. She wanted this man, as no other. Their attraction was startling, and they couldn't let go of each other. He encircled her, enveloped her, and she surrendered, leaning into him, her mouth open to his, every inch of their bodies touching.

He took her hand, no words spoken, and led her from the balcony to the bedroom, unfastening his tie as he went. Only one small lamp glowed in the corner of the room as he pulled her to the bed. He wrapped his arms tightly around her and began kissing her again. Without taking his mouth off hers, he unzipped her beautiful dress, while Suzy unbuttoned his shirt. Their kisses were deep and wet, their breathing heavy. Her hands touched his muscular chest, and her arms were around his neck. God, what was happening to her? Her dress slid to her ankles, and she gasped as he unfastened her bra. Max licked and gave lingering kisses to her delicate, perfectly proportioned breasts. Her dark nipples contrasted with her alabaster skin, and their taste turned him on. His mouth moved downward, his tongue tracing a line to the lacy edge of her red thong panties. He kept caressing her breasts, making Suzy feel out of control. Her pearlescent skin was beautiful. He began kissing her mouth as Suzy felt him hard against her. She began touching him, wanting him. He took his shirt and pants off, throwing them on the floor by her dress. Suzy and Max collapsed onto the bed, and he took her panties off and slid his tongue into her warm secret place. Her taste excited him, and she responded without any restraint. He undressed fully, spread her legs, and began rubbing his hardness against her opening, kissing her breasts, her mouth, loving her taste. He couldn't get enough of her. The warmth of his mouth on her nipples made her want him even more.

He touched her, his hand between her legs, his fingers exploring her, both wanting more, but she pushed him away, grasped him, and began licking and sucking his full male hardness, wanting and needing him inside of her. He couldn't wait any longer. He had to have her. Now. He entered her and gently but rhythmically made love to her. He was an adept lover and Suzy was craving his every move, every caress, every kiss, feeling his strong masculine chest against her breasts. She clung to him, feeling no inhibitions, only longing. He was part of her, his power lunging into her; holding her beautiful ass, he was pulling her against him with each thrust. Her heart pounded as his exquisite cock filled her, making her fall into the hypnotic trance of passionate love, and she began to moan, very low, whispering, "Max, oh Max," and he couldn't stop until they both came, his warmth flowing into her, neither thinking of anything but the now, this moment, and never wanting it to end.

# 6

Joey got to the Subway Office, Upper West Side, by 6:15 a.m. He had about fifteen minutes to spare. He clocked in and said good morning to the station manager.

"Hi, Marty," he said to his boss, who was sitting at his desk, head down, shoulders hunched, staring at his computer screen.

Joey wasn't sure how old Marty was, probably mid-fifties, but he knew the hours were long and Marty could get pretty stressed out. He complained a lot about the constant bureaucratic bullshit emails and endless reports he had to complete. Five maintenance staff worked this station and Marty had to write up any and all out of the ordinary events that occurred, plus maintain schedules for two other stations as well. When summer vacations started, his work load would get worse, but Joey and the other guys liked Marty and put up with his attitude. He and Marty were good friends and Joey knew Marty relied on him when any problem cropped up.

"How was your weekend?" Joey asked Marty.

Marty said, "The usual, how was yours?" Marty wasn't much for small talk, but was an okay boss. He left Joey alone, knowing

Joey was a responsible guy. He had to ride several of the others, so Joey did pretty well, just showing up and being there on time. Plus Joey didn't miss much, keeping his eye on the crowds, the rails, and keeping the place swept and orderly.

"It was a good weekend," Joey answered. "Did you see the game last night? Unbelievable. I didn't think they would win, and then Jeter hit it out of the park. The Yankees may have a chance to win the pennant this year."

Marty said, "Yeah, loved the game, but fell asleep after the seventh inning. Crap! I hate when I do that. Then I miss the best part. At least they won. I hate waking up to a blowout."

Joey put his lunch in his locker, poured some coffee into a Styrofoam cup, and then sat down in one of the chairs at the lunch table. He didn't have much time, but needed a bit more coffee to get him started.

"Sure is a hot June," Joey observed. "If the whole summer is like this, the city is going to be miserable, and the passengers are going to be a pain in the ass. It's going to mean more trouble with gang bangers and robberies and God knows what."

Marty said, "We just have to rely on the cops, and if you see anything out of the ordinary, just radio for help, and you'll get back up fast. The cops are always on patrol at most of the stations."

Joey said, "Yeah, I know, but five minutes can be a long time when I am in a face-off with a gang of punks and I don't have jack for protection."

Marty understood fully. Joey had been in several tussles with purse snatchers, drug users, and other assholes causing trouble. The police were diligent, but shit happens fast, and Joey knew it. He was a big guy though and had confidence. Other maintenance staff began to arrive as Joey finished his coffee. He headed out of the gray door that would take him to the steps leading to the platform. "Hey, fellas," and a few "Monday morning" comments were made in passing.

It was early, but that gave him some time to sweep, empty the trash bins, and do his routine safety check before crowds got really heavy. It was boring at times, but he liked staying busy and knew it was an important job. Anything thrown on the rails could be trouble, and he didn't want a problem on his watch.

Joey headed up the stairs to the platform from the lower level. At least it was a cool place to work, out of the summer heat. People were milling around, waiting for the next car.

"Another day at the salt mines," he thought.

# 7

The phone call came in to the main switchboard at the Manhattan Field Office of the FBI at exactly 8:00 a.m. that Monday morning. The call had been recorded, and the alert operator immediately informed her ranking supervisor, who contacted Special Agent Georgiana Reed. The NYC subway system was the target of a possible terrorist threat. The source was unknown, possibly a hoax, but all threatening calls were taken seriously.

Agent Reed reacted immediately and picked up the phone to call her partner, Mark Strickland. "Come to my office right away, Mark."

Georgiana's tone made it clear that this was no ordinary bullshit session. Mark was a fairly new agent at the Manhattan Field Office, early into his second year with the FBI, but he had ten years of experience on the NYPD. Georgiana recognized him as a proven asset and they worked well together. She felt lucky to have him as a partner.

When she and Mark listened to the playback, the menacing call sounded like the real deal, and George, as her staff called her, knew instinctively not to let this one pass.

The muffled male voice made it brief, uttering one sentence: "Subway hit today." The trace was to a public telephone in downtown Manhattan.

"Damn," she said, under her breath, looking at Mark.

They listened to the recording several times. George knew that the public telephone would offer no useful information, but she had to check it out anyway.

Georgiana was a tall, attractive redhead with green eyes. She was well known for her serious, take no shit attitude. An expert marksman, her Glock never left her hip. Both she and Mark were single, somewhat friendly, but stayed focused on their jobs. She met Mark when he was assigned to be her partner and liked him immediately. In fact, she liked him too much. She kept her feelings buried and maintained a strictly professional attitude toward him.

Georgiana was divorced, no kids, and had leftover scars from her brief marriage. She and Denny had been high school sweethearts and were still going together in college. He was the love of her life, but when George found out he had gone out with another girl, she was crushed and broke up with him. Several years after graduation, they ran into each other and reconnected. She fell for him again. She had never really gotten over him. They soon became engaged, and everything felt so right. He had a business degree, plus an MBA, and was working in marketing for a large corporation. George had a degree in criminal justice and was in training at the FBI when they got married. Everything felt so perfect, and she loved him with all of her heart and soul, but it hadn't taken long for her to realize he was the same old Denny. She had been in denial at first. He had to travel frequently on company business, and all the signs were there. After an ugly confrontation, he admitted he had been with someone else. His assertion that it meant nothing to him didn't work for her. The marriage was over.

She hoped the right man would come along some day. She put the job first and kept relationships on an impersonal level. Being a "loner" worked best for her, but in her heart, she needed love. For now, work filled the gaps.

Mark was single and didn't have much free time to date. His career was foremost right now, but he wanted marriage and a family someday. Being an agent was a high-risk profession requiring a lot of overtime hours. It would take the right woman to put up with the demands of his job. He was tall with dark brown hair and a dark shadow of beard. He trained hard to stay in shape, a habit he learned while working on the force.

His sexy appearance had not escaped George's notice. She sensed that he liked her but had to maintain a barrier. She often wondered how it would feel to have him hold her, but she forced herself "not to go there." It was at night, though, when she was struggling to fall asleep and feeling alone, that she imagined someone in bed next to her, holding her. In those moments, the only man she ever envisioned next to her was Mark.

# 8

Maggie entered Century Air crew scheduling, said hi to the guys as she signed in for Flight 227, and then went into the adjoining flight attendants' lounge. The chairs were full with FA's between flights or waiting out delays. She was an hour ahead of departure and saw the other four flight attendants from 227 had already checked in.

"Hey, Jackie, Mary Ann, how did your weekends go?" Maggie asked of both.

"Very hot but I enjoyed the days off," said Jackie.

"Me, too," said Mary Ann.

Maggie waved hello to the other crew members, Justin and Terry, who were also working 227.

After a quick chat, Maggie went into the supervisor's office to talk with Laura Cameron. She was not just her manager but a friend as well. She and Maggie had known each other for the ten years Maggie had flown for Century. Both had been around long enough to see many flight attendants come and go. Some flew only a few years and then left to get married or got tired of the pace.

The new regulations following 9/11, plus the increasing number of unruly passengers were frustrating, but Maggie was upbeat and found laughter was the best way to deal with the stresses of the job. And she loved flying. She enjoyed the friendships of the other crew members, and the pay and perks were unbeatable.

"Laura, how's everything is going?" asked Maggie. Laura was leaning down, putting her purse away in a desk drawer.

"Great, Maggie, how about Mike and the boys?" asked Laura, looking up as Maggie walked in.

Laura was around fifty, with blonde shoulder-length hair, worn in a stylish bob. She was strikingly pretty with a great figure. Having been a flight attendant when they were called stewardesses, she knew all facets of the job. She was old school and had the highest standards for all who worked for her and Century Air. She drove a black classic 300 ZX, taught classes to flight attendant trainees every other month, and always stopped to look up when she heard a plane overhead to see if it was a Century airliner. Flying was her life.

"They are fine. Mike and I had fun taking them to the park. We rode our bikes, but we mostly hung out. What did you do over the weekend?"

Laura replied, "I had a date." She had a pleased smile on her face.

"Oh, are you still seeing Bud?"

"Yes, he is truly amazing. We spent the whole weekend at his crash pad, alone. I'm falling for this guy, and it scares me." She laughed. Maggie knew Bud Wittwer, a Century Air captain, very good looking and recently divorced.

"He's a really great guy, Laura. I hope it works out."

Laura said, "We sure click in the bedroom, and I think he likes me. We can't keep our hands off each other. He's all I think about. He calls every day, and we have another date this weekend. I can hardly stand it. Horny doesn't cover it." They laughed. "He is my dream lover."

"Laura, it sounds wonderful. I'll keep my fingers crossed. Just let things happen, right?" smiled Maggie.

Laura said, "Yes, I'm letting things happen." She blushed. "I don't know why I keep buying sexy lingerie. It doesn't stay on very long."

Laughing, Maggie said, "I better get to the gate and start setting up. See you later, if you are still here when I get back. Flights are on schedule so far?" Maggie asked.

"Yes, the weather is good with no delays. Have a good one," said Laura.

"You, too. And let me know how the weekend goes with Bud," said Maggie.

"Oh, I will," said Laura, looking happy.

"Ciao!"

Maggie left the lounge, noticing that the other crew members were gone, so she hurried to the gate.

Before boarding, she checked with the gate agent, Steve, asking how many were on the flight.

He said, "So far, one hundred thirty-seven. Not too bad."

Maggie smiled and said, "Sounds like we'll be busy," and headed for the boarding ramp.

Steve couldn't talk further, as passengers were lining up, checking on their boarding passes. The MD 88 was her favorite equipment, and it was easy to work. With some unfilled seats, she and Terry would have extra time to assist the other crew members with the meal service, if necessary.

Since Maggie was senior, she had the responsibilities of doing all flight reports and assigning duties to the other flight attendants. They had worked this flight as a team for over eight months, so they knew the routine. They switched off when necessary and had formed close friendships, enjoying the pleasant camaraderie.

After stowing her gear in the first class coat closet, Maggie began the safety check of fire extinguishers, safety doors, slides, oxygen tanks, and first aid kit. She counted and signed off on the liquor and meal counts with the food service agent, and greeted the other FAs. The cockpit was empty. The captain and first officer were still doing their standard exterior visual safety check. Terry started the coffee and assisted the other crew members in the rear cabin.

Maggie sliced the lemons and limes for cocktails and made sure the warming ovens were turned on. She noted several extra meals and was glad there would be hot meals for the crew. A champagne brunch would be served to first class on white china with white cloth tray covers and napkins. She loved the elegant service, reminiscent of the earlier days of flying that she had heard about. Century was trying to bring deluxe service back on some of the longer flights. It was good PR, and the deluxe flights were popular and booked well in advance.

The captain and copilot came on board and began their routine preflight checklists. Maggie poured them each a cup of coffee in china mugs, one regular, one with cream.

"Morning, John, Allen."

"Hey, Maggie, thanks," said Captain John Wesley, as she handed them their coffee.

"Weather looks good for the trip. We'll try to keep it smooth for you," said Allen Delaney, the first officer, sitting to the right of the captain.

Maggie smiled. "Great, I will remind you that you said that!" She really liked them both. They were experienced, both former military pilots, and nice guys.

Boarding would begin in a few minutes, and she had nearly finished her preflight duties. Terry was working with her in first class, and Mary, Jackie, and Justin were working in business class. Terry walked up the aisle to join Maggie at the entrance of the plane. It was nearly time for boarding.

She said to Maggie, "How are you?" She thought Maggie wasn't her usual self but wasn't sure.

"Okay, I think. I hope I am not getting a bug," answered Maggie.

Terry and Maggie had been friends and coworkers for many years. Terry Jamison was a senior flight attendant, as well, with just a few years less experience than Maggie. Terry was pretty, single, and knew the ropes. They felt a sisterly kinship, and Maggie enjoyed hearing about Terry's single lifestyle. Terry knew Maggie's family and loved her boys. They always bid the same flight and were glad to get to work together.

Terry gave Maggie a hug and said, "Let me know if you start to feel worse."

She was a little concerned. Terry walked back to her position at mid-cabin.

Suddenly, Maggie felt nauseated, just for a moment, but then it passed. She hoped it was just the lack of breakfast, but she also felt dizzy. She tried to shake it off. She went to the galley and opened a small carton of orange juice, hoping that would help.

The gate agent, Steve, walked down the ramp to the open door where Maggie was waiting and said, "You ready, Maggie?" He noticed Maggie looked a little shaky and pale as she stood leaning against the bulkhead, drinking from the carton.

She said, "Sure, send them on."

He stepped inside the doorway of the plane and asked with concern, "Are you sure?"

She brushed the feelings off best she could. "Yes, I'll be fine, thanks. It must be the heat or something." She touched her brow.

He said, "Okay, but if you want, I can call for a sub. It isn't too late. You have a long day ahead, and it is a nearly full list."

"Thanks, but I'll get through. Maybe something I ate." She smiled but inwardly had some doubts. She hoped it was nothing.

"All right, Maggie. We're going to start boarding."

Maggie said, "We're ready," throwing the carton into the trash, forcing herself into her best "meet and greet" position.

On more than one occasion, she had worked when sick. She could do it again, if necessary. Terry was great to work with and would step in if she got sick. Terry was standing near the business class entrance, ready to direct passengers to their seats and help stow carry-on luggage in the overhead compartments.

"Good morning," said Maggie as the first two passengers came on board.

They smiled back and said, "Good morning." It was business as usual, except for the queasiness that was becoming harder for Maggie to ignore.

# 9

Joey came out of the storage closet with trash bags, dustpan, and broom. He grabbed a pair of rubber gloves, out of habit, and put them on. He started along the back wall, eyeing the comings and goings of the crowd, on their way to work. He was often envious, thinking they had better jobs and more exciting lives, but he tried to think positively. He recognized some of the regulars, especially the pretty girls. He saw the blonde flight attendant get on the train, and whistled under his breath. She was "hot." He loved summer, "short skirt season," when he could check out her sexy legs. He better put those horny thoughts away until tonight; he smiled to himself.

As Joey surveyed the area, he noticed some debris on the track and took the small concrete staircase down to pick it up. It was just some paper cups and napkins. He kept looking while down there. It was early, and there wasn't much to pick up after a quiet Sunday night.

He climbed out of the track area and surveyed the already bustling station. He walked toward the rear of platform, noticing out of the corner of his eye, an object behind one of the support pillars, barely visible. It appeared to be a canister, like the kind that cleaning sprays come in, only taller and narrower. It was dark gray with no markings and no lid. He leaned over to pick it up and noticed it had some moisture on it. It was probably nothing. He threw it into the garbage bag and headed for the storage closet to return his supplies and put the trash bag in the large trash can, along with his rubber gloves. Glad that's done. He would have to clean again before he left his post, but no big deal. Joey's main job was to monitor the passengers as subway trains came and went. He had a radio in case of emergencies. The police were always nearby, and he could check in with Marty, if necessary.

Joey's thoughts wandered back to the dark gray canister. Something about it bothered him. It was the norm to find all kinds of junk, trash, personal objects, like combs, cigarette lighters, watches, and all kinds of weird stuff, but ever since the 9/11 terrorist attack, he had become wary of anything out of the ordinary. Just for the hell of it, he stepped into a more quiet area of the station and radioed Marty.

Marty instantly answered, "What's up, Joey?"

"Probably nothing, but I found an odd looking canister, no lid, no label, with some moisture on the outside of it, and I disposed of it in the trash. Thought I better report it."

"Did it smell like anything, window cleaner or something?" asked Marty.

Joey said, "No, I didn't smell it. It just seemed odd to me—that's all. Plus the fact that it was sitting in a dark corner, behind a support beam."

Marty said, "I'll key it in as a "suspicious object report." Maybe keep track of the bag it's in so it doesn't get away from us, just in case, if you know what I mean."

"Yeah, CYA time," said Joey.

Joey knew Marty took him seriously, and neither one let anything slip by them, just in case. They had to be extra cautious with any small thing, which normally turned out to be nothing. But who could be sure? Anyway, Joey signed off with Marty. He kept thinking of the canister, though, and hoped it was nothing. He was glad he remembered to wear the rubber gloves.

It was about 8:30 a.m., that hot June Monday morning, when Marty looked up and saw two uniformed NYPD cops walk into the office.

# 10

Georgiana grabbed the phone. Her voice never wavered as she gave instructions to the field office on-call team to check out the public phone from which the "terrorist's" call had been placed and to notify the New York City Metropolitan Transit Authority and the chief of police. George, having gotten the ball rolling, called Manhattan FBI Field Office Director, Fran Jacobs, filling her in on the few details she knew. George had met Director Jacobs at the FBI Academy. Fran had been one of her instructors and they had become friends. Fran had confidence in George's capabilities to take the lead on this one.

Her next call was to the Department of Homeland Security, asking to speak to the regional director, Tom Bennett. Mark was listening, taking notes, as Georgiana introduced herself, and began informing Director Bennett of the possible threat to the NYC subway system. He asked George to mobilize the FBI Counterterrorism Task Force as a precaution, and he would alert the Mayor, as well as the New York State National Guard. She told Bennett that the NYPD was currently on scene, and they would be first responders. Her agents, part of the Task Force, would get there soon and do a thorough investigation. There would be no "turf war" only teamwork, especially in the aftermath of 9/11.

Director Bennett said, "Please keep me informed of any potential threat."

As she hung up, she said to Mark, "Grab some coffee. It may take a while for things to start happening, if this isn't a hoax. Let's hope it is." George made the necessary phone calls as Bennett had directed, and now it was a tension-filled "waiting game."

Mark, dressed in khakis and a light blue dress shirt with sleeves rolled up, solid navy tie with miniature white polka dots, Glock in his shoulder holster, headed to the half-filled coffee pot. The coffee smelled fresh enough, so he grabbed a clean mug and poured himself a cup. Then he sat down in the worn but comfortable chair across from George. He threw his navy sport coat over the arm of the other chair. He was outwardly relaxed and composed, but she knew his mind was going through multiple scenarios, as was hers. Their eyes met, but neither spoke.

Mark noted the time. It was 8:20 a.m. He watched George walk to the window and knew what she was thinking. His vivid memories of 9/11 wouldn't go away either. He and his NYPD partner had been among the first responders. They had entered the North Tower and Jimmy had followed Mark up the stairs. The heat and flames were un-fucking-believable. Mark lost count of how many he carried out. Overtaken by smoke and fumes, he had to be treated for smoke inhalation and exhaustion. He never saw Jimmy again. He vowed that day to be at the front end of the problem, never again the back end, making certain there would never be another 9/11.

Mark loved watching Georgiana, her sensual curves visible through the pale silk blouse, softly patterned, golden tones over beige, which matched the dark brown fitted slacks, with the faintest trace of her bikini panty lines showing. The colors were the perfect complement to her long red hair. The flowing fabric hugged her sexy figure, adding to the attraction. Her beige low heels were classic and practical. He knew she had a small pistol strapped to her ankle, and the Glock was in a paddle holster on her hip. The PPK in her purse was a backup. Sweet, he thought. He would tell her soon how he felt, but not now.

Fifteen minutes later, they got the report. No evidence was found on the phone booth, but two police officers were at the scene where the "suspicious object" had been discovered. It was placed in a sealed evidence bag. The Metropolitan Transit Authority had shut down the subway system temporarily, as a precaution. The police officers were questioning the station manager and the subway inspector. The maintenance worker had noticed the odd canister and instinctively knew to set it aside, "in case." He appeared nervous but not suspiciously so. Joey Caruso had been ruled out as a suspect after a quick background check. They worked fast.

George made the necessary calls, grabbed her purse and brown suit jacket from the back of the door, and said, "Let's go. We can take your car."

Mark drove a black Mustang GT, perfect fit for him. He grabbed his jacket, following her out the door, both hoping for a boring and uninteresting day.

# II

After reaching cruising altitude, Maggie and Terry began the brunch service. They heard the familiar double chime that meant the flight crew wanted to speak to a cabin attendant.

Maggie picked up the intercom, and Captain Wesley said, "Maggie, please come to the cockpit."

"Yes, John, I'll be right there."

This must be important, thought Maggie. Her head was still throbbing, and the nausea and dizziness were getting harder to ignore. The ibuprofen she had taken had not helped. She walked back to the beverage cart where Terry was busy with the morning beverage service of Mimosas, champagne cocktails, Bloody Marys, orange juice, and coffee.

"I need to speak to the crew. I'll be right back," she whispered to Terry. They exchanged questioning glances since this was a rare occurrence.

"Sure, Maggie."

The ride had been smooth, with no storms or turbulence. "Oh well," thought Terry, "It's probably nothing." She resumed serving, handing a flute of sparkling champagne to a passenger.

Maggie, on the other hand, wasn't sure. She went to the cockpit door and knocked twice—the code well known to the crew—and the door opened.

Maggie stepped into the cockpit, closed the door, and leaned forward, saying, "What's going on?"

Captain Wesley said, "We just received a report that all the New York City subways are temporarily shut down due to a terrorist threat."

"Oh my gosh!" exclaimed Maggie. "Is this for real?"

She was glad Mike didn't have to use the subway to get the boys to school, but her mind raced through other possibilities that were chilling.

"The Mayor said this was just a precaution, but he had to take it seriously, in case it turns out to be legitimate. You know how it is."

John tried to be reassuring when he realized she was alarmed. "There are lots of kooks that get their jollies scaring people. I just thought you should know. If a passenger picks up something off their Wi-Fi connection, we need to have a ready response. We haven't gotten word yet from the powers that be whether to announce or not. I wanted you and the crew to be on top of this. Just answer, if questioned, that it is a probable hoax, that we know nothing official, which is true, and that we will report any further information when it becomes available."

"That sounds plausible, John. I hope you are right." Maggie continued, "I was on the subway this morning. Glad I made it before it was shut down." She had pulled down the jump seat as they were talking and began rubbing her temples with her eyes closed.

"Are you feeling well?" asked Allen. "You look a little pale."

She responded, "I am not sure. I feel a little dizzy and queasy. I may be getting a flu bug or something. It started suddenly. I was fine until we started boarding. I thought it would go away."

Allen said, "Are you sure you can work? You can just sit it out if necessary."

"Thanks, Allen, but I am going to try to get through this. We are pretty busy, but we have a few empty seats if I get worse."

As she spoke the words, she really wasn't sure. She had never felt quite like this before.

"You let us know," said Captain Wesley, "and we will do whatever we can to help you."

He didn't like the way she was looking. It was obvious she was not well. Her color was off, and she looked shaky.

"You can curl up in a blanket in the back row and rest," John suggested.

That was tempting, but she forced a smile, stood up, and said, "I'd better get back and tell the others about the subway threat. The questions may have already started. Thanks, guys."

She opened the cockpit door, closed it, and heard the lock engage. Terry was in the galley, placing the used glassware in the metal storage bins. She started checking the warming trays in preparation for the meal service.

As she entered the kitchen, Maggie said, "Terry, you won't believe this. The subway system in the city is shut down due to a terrorist threat of some kind."

"Holy shit," whispered Terry, her eyes widened. "Oh, I am sorry. But you know what I mean. What is going on?" Terry looked genuinely worried.

Maggie quietly responded, "I don't know, probably nothing, but they have to be sure. You know how it is."

"You're right. It's probably a crank."

Maggie didn't hear Terry's remarks. She had crumpled to the floor, unconscious.

# 12

In January, after a long day at work, Suzy pulled her Lexus into her garage and unlocked the door to her elegant townhouse. It was located in the exclusive Edgewood gated community called The Bayside Retreat. The much sought after property was tucked away in a beautiful wooded area, with walking trails, a large, well-equipped gym, a community room, and indoor and outdoor swimming pools. The townhouses were all brick colonial with lovely well-maintained gardens.

After walking in through the kitchen, she noticed a manila envelope lying on the hardwood floor near the front door. Suzy bent over and picked it up. There was no writing on the envelope.

"Strange," she thought. It was most likely some ad or information from a real estate agent who had somehow gotten access after an appointment with another resident. The upscale community was on the list of the most desirable places to live due to its convenience, privacy, and amenities.

Suzy placed her purse and keys on the hall table in the foyer and opened the envelope, not sure what to expect. She was jolted by the typed cryptic message on a plain white sheet of paper. She knew it would come, but somehow, she was still caught off guard. The information was concise and clear in its instructions. It was signed, in type, "The Organization."

There was no wiggle room. She had agreed to their terms, knew the risks, but still had not wrapped her thoughts fully around the mission. Her self-discipline would eventually allow her to complete her task. The rewards were significant, and she had been carefully chosen due to a variety of factors. They had been brilliant in in their selection of Dr. Suzy Chen. Unknown to her, she had been under scrutiny since her days as a coed at the University of Delaware. With impeccable credentials, graduating at the top of her class, getting her PhD in pharmacology and with a stellar recommendation from her superior at the pharmaceutical company where she had worked for five years, she easily landed her position in research and development at the Edgewood Arsenal.

She had her motives, and the Organization had theirs. The blend was perfect. If caught, the price was high, but she had some protection, operating with the help of this secret underground directive. Her skills were valuable to them, and they knew she needed them, as well.

She went into her office on the first floor and unlocked the top desk drawer, She paused only a moment to pick up the two yellowed photos, stare at them purposefully, and then carefully placed them back in the drawer, along with the sealed manila envelope containing the letter. She locked the drawer. Suzy exhaled, tried to shake off her racing thoughts and nervous reaction, and then began her usual at home routine. She changed out of her work clothes and into black running tights, a cotton turtleneck, and white sweatshirt. She would jog to unwind and then have dinner, something frozen, as she formulated her role in the plan and how she would implement it without discovery. She also thought of Max and her overwhelming love and desire for him. Their affair was still new, but images of him filled all her waking moments. They had a date Friday night, only one more night to wait. She knew he felt the same about her, but his job kept him in DC most of the week. She thought only of him as she stepped out of the side door, off the garage, bending to do some light stretching before she started off on her run. She enjoyed the cool temperatures, saw her breath in the air, and then her mind wandered to what she would wear tomorrow night. But the letter began to dominate her thoughts, and she mentally outlined the steps she would take, excited to begin the project. The exhilaration pumped her up. Suzy began a steady quick pace and finished her three-mile run, breathlessly, in record time.

# 13

Mike woke the boys and reminded them to wash their hands and faces, comb their hair, and get dressed. They were ages four and six and enjoyed the days spent with just their dad. They dressed in the clothes their mom had laid out for them—cute navy slacks, white polo shirts, and their favorite cool tennis shoes. All the students at Pembrooke Academy followed the dress code. It was tradition, and the polo shirts had the Pembrooke logo on the front. They felt special and grown up in their school clothes, aware that it was a really neat school. The girls at Pembrooke wore white blouses or pretty white T-shirts and navy Capri slacks or skirts.

Tim was the youngest and very bright, thoughtful, and a bit reserved. Mike Jr., also quite smart, was already acting as the older brother. He watched out for his younger brother, with no rivalry between them. Mike and Maggie loved their boys so much and were proud of them. They were kind and considerate and academically advanced for their ages. Maggie was sure they got their intelligence from their dad, but Mike assured Maggie that she was the smart one. Maggie had done well in college, getting her business

degree at the University of Maryland. Mike had gotten his gradu-
ate degree there, and that was where they met. He was three years
older, and Maggie had quickly fallen for this sexy grad student. He
had seen her on campus and made sure to run into her as often as
possible, in the student union, cafeteria, or library. He was captivated as well, and after some casual dates, both were sure of their
love, and their chemistry was undeniable.

Mike had prepared their favorite breakfast of instant oat-
meal with fresh berries. Plus they loved pop tarts and had one each
morning with their milk. The boys had diligently combed their
hair and washed their faces. Their good behavior was a result of
the great love and gentle discipline of their parents, plus a reflection of what they had learned over and above their studies at the
Academy.

"Okay guys, brush your teeth, and we'll leave," he said, seeing
they had finished eating, and were taking their cereal bowls to the
sink.

They rushed off to their bathroom and were soon out and
ready to go, back packs in hand. Mike had on khaki cargo shorts
and a T-shirt and was ready for the short walk to school. The boys
enjoyed the camaraderie of the "guy talk" as they made their way
to Pembrooke and were interested in the baseball game last night.
Mike assured them he had recorded it, and they could watch it
tonight. They loved the Yankees and couldn't wait to attend a game
this season, as their dad had promised.

They ran off, waving good-bye, after reaching the school's
gated entrance, and Mike began the walk home, looking forward
to his coffee and bagel. It sure was hot, and he was glad he wore
shorts. He got to the coffee shop, a bit crowded, waited in line for
his café latte and bagel, and then sat at one of the small empty
tables by the window to read the paper, relax a little in the cool

air-conditioning, and listen to the news on the TV mounted above one corner of the shop. He put the paper down to listen to the sports report from last night. He had missed the end of the game. Jeter had hit another one!

"The boys will love seeing that replay," he thought.

He and Maggie had gone to bed soon after putting the boys to bed. They knew they had to rise early, and they weren't night owls anyway. Warm thoughts of Maggie were brilliant images in his mind, and he imagined she was probably already at the airport, getting ready for her flight. He never worried for her safety, but he was always glad when she got home.

Mike finished his bagel and walked home, sipping the rest of his coffee. He had work piled on his desk and began to mentally outline his day. He had the discipline to work in the home environment, and his office was strictly off limits to the family. He had many projects, including some articles to edit. They were fascinating to him. He often wanted to do actual research, not just read about studies that others were doing in various fields. He let himself into the apartment, did a quick kitchen cleanup, started brewing some coffee, and walked down the hall to his office. He turned on the radio, just for background music, opened his laptop, and began his day.

# 14

None of the passengers could see Maggie on the floor in the forward galley. Terry opened the First Class coat closet and found the first aid kit, strapped to the right side bulkhead. She grabbed it, along with a pillow and blanket, and then she rushed back to Maggie, who looked like she was in a troubled sleep, sweat on her brow. She placed the pillow under Maggie's head and the blanket over her. She placed a cool towel on Maggie's forehead and checked her breathing and pulse. Both were steady but rapid. She tried speaking to her, but there was no response.

Terry picked up the intercom and rang Captain Wesley. "Yes, Terry. What's up?"

"John, we have a problem. Maggie is unconscious, passed out in the forward galley."

"I am sending Allen out," John answered.

"Thanks."

Allen came out of the cockpit, walked the few short steps to the galley, and knelt down beside Maggie. He checked her pulse, listened to her breathing and tried the amyl nitrate, which he found in the first aid kit. There was little response. Maggie moved her head slightly, but didn't wake up. He and Terry looked at each other, both deeply concerned.

Allen spoke first. "I'll notify Captain Wesley and let you know. We may turn around or make an emergency landing at the first possible airport. We are nearing BWI. Let the aft crew know what's going on. We'll make an announcement about the intermediate stop, and you find out if there is a doctor on board."

Terry nodded. "Okay." She picked up the intercom handset, her hand trembling.

# 15

The ringing telephone woke Dave and Chris. It was around 9:30 a.m., and they were still wrapped in each other's arms on the office sofa. Dave got to the phone first, in case his wife was calling. He would have a good excuse for working past his shift and he wanted to protect Chris if possible, though, at this point, almost everyone knew they were lovers. It was Dr. Frank Edwards, one of the daylight shift ER physicians.

"Sorry, Dave, did I wake you?" asked Edwards.

"That's okay, Frank. What's going on?" asked Dave, on alert quickly.

Dr. Edwards spoke with directness, "There has been a terror ist threat to the subway, and the Mayor shut down the entire system. An investigation is underway, and all hospitals and medical facilities have been notified, in case patients arrive with unusual symptoms. We are being asked to note if there is any commonality of their symptoms. Also, we are to ask them if they had used the subway station in question, and so forth. A suspicious object was found at an Express Subway Station, and it is currently being transported by air to the FBI lab at Quantico. The CDC has been notified, as well."

Dave hesitated and then spoke, "I will stay on duty as backup and will alert the hospital administrator in case we need extra staff."

Frank appreciated the offer and said "Thanks, Dave. I hope we don't have to deal with anything out of the ordinary. I guess in this city, that is considered routine," he said with a laugh.

Grant agreed, "You can say that again," thinking of some of the bizarre incidents he had observed since he moved to New York.

He redirected his thoughts. "Call me if anything comes up. I am going to order some breakfast and will be here in the office."

After Dave explained to Chris what Dr. Edwards had said, she asked, "Shall I stay?"

She had gotten dressed while he was on the phone and felt unusually nervous about the call. There had been alerts before, but this felt different. She sensed that Dave thought so as well.

He said, "Let me call the staff lunchroom and order some breakfast, and we can wait for a short while and may know something soon. I hate to leave, face a long commute, and have to come back again."

He followed her questioning look with, "Yes, call the on-duty charge nurse, and let her know you are here."

Chris knew Connie and felt comfortable talking with her, especially in her current compromising situation.

Connie answered from the desk, "Hi, Chris, I didn't know you were here. Guess you had a long night, but you and your staff did a good job tying up the loose ends on all the patients. Those that had been waiting for admission are now in their assigned rooms. The cardiac patient is in ICU. Dr. Stone will see him this morning. Most have been sent home, stitched, or whatever. We have had several more arrive in the meantime, nothing unusual so far."

"It's all yours, but call me either in Dave's office or on my cell phone. We are going to have breakfast then maybe we will know something after that. Did you have trouble getting to work?" asked Chris.

"Hell, yes. It was a nightmare, but thankfully I caught a bus, which was packed, but I got here okay. Traffic is a mess, but fortunately most people got to work before the shutdown. Living in the city is a daily pain in the ass, even without a crisis, right?" said Connie, with her wry sense of humor.

"So true," Chris said in agreement. "Keep us informed. I'll let you know when I am leaving."

Dave and Chris were finishing their toast, cereal, and orange juice when Dave's phone rang.

# 16

eorge had directed her agents, already on the scene, to isolate the station in question, with no one but authorized personnel allowed in or out. George and Mark were in phone contact with those inside the station manager's office and those on the platform. All FBI agents in the area in question were wearing special breathing masks with hoods for protection against any dangerous airborne contaminants, including chemical, biological, radiological, or nuclear. Additionally, they were fully armed. George had spoken to Regional Homeland Security Director, Tom Bennett, several times, assuring him that she would call the moment they knew anything further.

A sweep of the area had been completed, and the canister and bag in which it had been discarded had been placed in a secure biohazard container and was en route by chopper to the FBI Laboratory Services in Quantico, Virginia. The FBI lab had a quick response team that specialized in forensic science, including chemical, biological, explosive, and various hazardous materials. The FBI investigating team was gathering samples from the subway platform, placing them in sealed bags, to ascertain whether any weapons grade agent contamination was present.

Marty, Joey, and the other subway workers who were on duty at the time of discovery were instructed to remain in the station office and wait until further notice. The few passengers who had been waiting on the platform were mingling, talking in low tones to each other or on cell phones, calling their workplace, office, or family and friends, alarmed and scared, seeing these masked figures swabbing the area and doing whatever they were doing. It looked like a scene out of a bad science fiction movie.

Joey was feeling so frightened, somewhat queasy, and nervous about what was happening. He called Donna, knowing that she probably had been watching the news, and explained that it was just an "unknown spray can or something," and that it was a precautionary shutdown.

He admitted that he was a little upset, and she said, "It is probably nothing, Joey," but she didn't want him to worry or know how concerned she was.

"Kiss Rosa for me," he asked.

Donna said, "I will. I love you, Joey."

"You too, sweetheart."

After the call, Joey walked over to Marty, who was getting some coffee, and said, "Hey, Marty, what do you think is going on?"

Marty held the warm cup in his hands and said, "Dunno, Joey, but I don't like it."

Joey said, "Me either, and honestly, I'm not feeling so good."

"What do you mean?" Marty looked Joey square in the face and saw that he was pale and sweating a lot.

"I am sick at my stomach and feel crummy. Maybe it is my nerves."

Marty said, "Look, have a cup of tea. That settles my stomach. Just go relax on the couch. All this craziness makes me edgy, too. Plus, I gotta report on all this shit. Just take it easy. We are all feeling the pressure."

Joey said, "Sure, Marty." He didn't think the tea would help, but he would give it a shot.

Joey saw the box of teabags, grabbed one, and filled a mug with hot water from the industrial sized urn. He dropped the teabag in the cup, grabbed a packet of soda crackers, and headed to the couch. He was glad to get off his feet. One of the other workers was there, waiting like the rest of them.

"Hey, Eddie, how are you feeling?" asked Joey.

Eddie was impatient and said, "I am sick of waiting and not knowing what is going on."

His eyes were glued to the small TV, sitting on an old card table against the wall across from them. Other guys were watching too, sitting in chairs, scattered around the crowded, stuffy office. Occasionally there would be a news bulletin about the subway shutdown, and there was a steady crawl of information going across the bottom of the screen, with the announcement of Breaking News highlighted in yellow.

Eddie heard the cup hit the floor, shatter, and hot tea splattered on his feet.

"Shit, man, look what you did, asshole." Then he saw Joey tumble sideways, falling off the couch, hitting his head on the worn brown carpet, landing on the broken cup, his vomit mixing with the wet tea stain.

# 17

F t. Detrick, in Maryland, code name, Area A, conducts biomedi-
cal research and is home to the Bio-Defense Agency, the US
Army Medical Research and Material Command, and the US
Army Medical Research Institute of Infectious Diseases. Most
Americans don't know of its purpose or even its existence.

All biological weaponry is initially evaluated at Ft. Detrick and
is then transported to the Aberdeen Proving Ground for testing and
development of "Collective Protection Systems." The deadly samples
are safely stored in a special "security access only" containment lab,
located at the Edgewood Laboratory facility at the APG. The Edgewood lab, the Edgewood Chemical and Biological Center, is run
by the military, and security is stringent, especially since 9/11. The
deliveries of weapon grade agents normally occur at one a.m. when
the building is empty except for skeleton staff members and military
police. These items are received by assigned chemists, expert in the
handling and storage of these lethal toxins and bio-agents.

The deadly agents are obtained from various places, often
from combat zones or other sources, such as foreign terrorist cells.

Numerous "Weapons of Mass Destruction" were discovered in Iraq after the overthrow of Saddam Hussein, but the knowledge of the recovery operation was top secret. The development of toxins and biological weapons is also a role of the Edgewood Laboratories, but this is highly classified. Due to all of its functions, the Edgewood Lab would be a perfect target. Therefore, the highest levels of security are mandatory.

Dr. Suzy Chen, as assistant director of research and development, in charge of Edgewood testing procedures, had often been present to receive the transfers from Detrick to the Edgewood lab facility. She would, as required by safety standard operating procedures, wear proper full hooded protection during these transfers. Several months earlier she had formulated her plan, so she knew which specimens were being delivered and when. She had arranged to be on duty the night a certain "item" was being transferred. She had arrived early and went to the storage room where the Level A Protective Suits were kept. The hooded gear was cumbersome, especially with the attached air supply breathing apparatus, but it was necessary. After suiting up, she walked to the loading dock. She waited nervously and heard the exchange of radio messages coordinating the arrival of the truck from Detrick. She heard loud beeping as the delivery truck backed up to the loading ramp and one of the regular armed military guards raised the large door that opened onto the dock. She nodded to the driver and said hello to his partner as he moved the sturdy wheeled cart off the truck ramp and inside the building.

"Thanks," said Suzy to Bob, one of the regular delivery personnel.

He got back into the unmarked truck, and the guard closed the doors. Easy does it, she said to herself. She had maintained her professional but friendly demeanor, and with great caution, she moved the wheeled cart from the guarded loading dock to the storage facility on the ground floor of the main building, which also housed the extensive secured laboratory. Two military guards accompanied her to the lab and then returned to their post at the delivery site. Armed guards were posted at the entrance doors to the lab as well.

Under the suit, around her waist, was hidden a small Velcro sealed pouch with a duplicate container. The "phonied" vial was ready for exchange with the "hot" vial. All she needed was one vial of the deadly Viral Agent X. All the vials had been safely sealed for transport. As planned, her clandestine work would begin soon. She only needed to work on the delivery system and felt confident that she could manage that easily. Her lab at home was small but well equipped, and she could handle the process.

She followed normal procedure, unlocking the cooled containment room, and she quickly placed the vials in their prepared and marked chemical biohazard storage unit. No one had seen her slip one vial of Agent X under her suit and replace it with the phony. She was aware of the hidden cameras and knew the angle necessary to camouflage the exchange.

"Done," she exclaimed to herself, with a self-satisfied exhalation.

Agent X had been transported, chilled in the -78.5 degrees C with dry ice. Her plan for getting the vial out of Edgewood involved secreting it in an ordinary thermos until she could get it into cold storage in the small laboratory in the locked closet of her condominium basement.

# 18

Suzy had invited Max for dinner that Friday night in March, and it was understood that they would spend the weekend together. That is how it had been since they had started dating several months ago. She delighted in preparing meals for him, such as the one she was serving tonight. The candlelight dinner would include his favorites: filet mignon with Béarnaise sauce, au gratin potatoes, grilled asparagus tips, and a fresh garden salad with homemade blue cheese dressing. There were soft rolls with butter, and for dessert, assorted pastries and miniature cheesecakes with fresh strawberries. He was bringing a Chilean merlot, and of course, their favorite aperitif, Grand Marnier.

She timed the meal perfectly and had most everything ready except for the steaks and asparagus. Those would be grilled at the last minute. The potatoes were warming in the oven, the salad was in the refrigerator, and her table was set beautifully, with a lovely mixed floral bouquet and sparkling crystal candleholders with white tapers that matched the damask tablecloth and napkins.

After a warm shower, Suzy dressed in her sexiest black lace thong panties and black strapless demi-cup bra, black capris, and a white off the shoulder cashmere sweater with three-quarter length sleeves. Diamond drop earrings were her only jewelry and they shimmered against her long black hair. Black spiked heels completed her ensemble. She loved dressing for him. After adding red lipstick and heavy eyeliner and mascara to accentuate her exotic almond eyes, she touched perfume to her wrists and cleavage. Now she just had to double check on dinner and wait for him. She was breathless and couldn't believe this wonderful man was in her life.

Suzy was impatient to see Max. She wanted to feel his touch and his mouth on hers. He was all she could think about every moment of each day. He should arrive soon but Suzy knew traffic was heavy on Fridays with commuters leaving Washington. The drive would probably take at least an hour and a half.

Suzy's cell phone rang and she saw it was Max.

"Hey, baby. Where are you?" she asked. She was so happy to hear his voice.

"I'm just punching in the security code at the entrance. I'll be there in a few minutes," he said.

"Hurry," she said, and hung up.

As she opened the door, he couldn't restrain from embracing her, his arms so tight around her, his mouth on hers, his tongue in her mouth, and she gave herself to him completely. Their deep wet kisses heightened their desire. He slid his hand under her sweater, touching her firm round breasts. Still holding her, he leaned against the front door to close it. He kept his mouth on hers, licking her lips, sucking her tongue, devouring her as he unzipped her capris and slid them off. He pushed her hard against the wall. His kisses could make her come, but she wanted to feel him inside her.

She kept saying, "Max, I want you, now."

Max whispered, "I want you, baby."

He was out of control. He ripped her panties off, unzipped his pants, and lifted her, her legs wrapped around his waist. He entered her, both of them panting. He moved inside of her, and she responded, and moved against him with each thrust, until they both reached their peaks of desire. Neither wanted to let go or stop. She felt his hot liquid inside her and loved that part of him that was now part of her. She knew she was his for the taking, now and forever. They stayed together, with lingering kisses, sliding to the floor. He was tender, loving, kissing her, telling her she was his, and no one could touch her but him, ever. She belonged to him.

Later, after their sumptuous candlelit meal, they sat nestled close together in her cozy den, sipping the richness of the Grand Marnier, while listening to classical music. They were learning about each other's backgrounds, and Suzy told him about her heritage, her early years with her family, the trips they made to Hong Kong, and why she had pursued her career path. Max was a bit older, almost twelve years, but it made no difference. He was all she wanted, a steady hand at the helm of her unsteady life. She hoped he would never let go.

# 19

The phone rang, startling Mike. He had been concentrating on the article he was editing for *Science Today* magazine.

He picked up his cell phone. "Mike Ryan speaking."

"Mr. Ryan, this is Jane Phillips, head nurse at Johns Hopkins University Hospital emergency room in Baltimore." Mike was familiar with the world-renowned teaching hospital and biomedical research facility.

Mike quickly responded. "Yes, how can I help you?" he asked, thinking it was a call about his recent article on stem cell research.

"Mr. Ryan, your wife, Maggie, has been admitted, and we would like your permission to treat her," she said.

Mike, shocked, exclaimed, "There's some mistake. My wife, a flight attendant, is working a flight to Miami. You must have another patient by that name."

"No, Mr. Ryan, your wife became ill on the flight. The plane made an unscheduled landing in Baltimore, and she was transported to our facility for treatment. She is currently stable, but unconscious, and has many symptoms that resemble a severe virus. Century Air operations will be calling you shortly, but they wanted to get her treated and made the quick decision to bring her here before placing calls. It all happened suddenly. Her flight has continued on to Miami, and the crew will call you upon arrival. They knew you would be very concerned."

"Please tell me what is going on." He was standing, becoming quite upset.

"Mr. Ryan," Nurse Phillips continued, "your wife is getting the best care possible. She is in isolation since we aren't sure if she is contagious. We are running tests, and we have an excellent team of doctors and nurses taking care of her." Her voice was reassuring, and Mike was beginning to feel less anxious. "Is there any medical history we need to know about, and is she currently taking any medications?"

He answered, "No, nothing. She has always been very healthy." His voice trailed off. "I need to get there. I will leave right away and be there as soon as possible," he said.

She told him where to find Maggie at the hospital.

"Please don't worry. At this point, it may be a matter of dehydration, low blood sugar, or anything. I know it is difficult to comprehend at this point, but being calm is best for you and your wife until we have more facts."

"Of course, you are right." He began to process what she had said. "We have two boys in school. I will arrange for our sitter to pick them up and then get there as soon as I can. Please call me if there is any news of her condition."

As he hung up, he got another call. It was Century crew scheduling, chief of operations, Dwight Hatfield, a familiar voice, since he would often call Maggie if there was a schedule change or if she was "on call" to fill in when another FA couldn't make his or her flight.

"Mike, this is Hatfield."

"Yes, Dwight. I just heard. What happened?" he asked.

"Maggie fainted, and John Wesley made the decision to land at BWI, just to make sure she's okay. There was a pediatrician on board, who checked her over, but he felt she needed to get to a hospital quickly, in case her condition suddenly deteriorated," he explained.

"Nothing else? Are you sure, Dwight?" asked Mike, his stomach tightening.

"That's it, Mike. You know what I know. John made the decision, and you know him. He is cautious and won't take chances, so it is probably nothing. He values his crew and felt it was in everyone's best interest to get Maggie checked out." Dwight was reassuring.

"Gotcha," said Mike. "I am going to Baltimore now, so I will let you all know."

"Thanks," said Dwight, knowing that he and the crew would be following up on Maggie's status anyway.

Thankfully, Mike reached the sitter, Annie, who lived in their building and frequently babysat for them.

She loved the boys, and they loved her. He called the school to notify the administration so the boys would be aware that Annie would be waiting to walk them home. He didn't give any details so that Mike and Tim wouldn't be upset. Until he knew what was going on, he was going to keep things calm, but he was anything but calm. His thoughts went to the terrorist threat of the NYC subway system, and Mike prayed to God that it had nothing to do with Maggie's illness.

# 20

eorgiana's cell phone rang. She and Mark were sitting in his Mustang, parked by the curb, about twenty-five yards from the subway entrance. It was one of their agents, calling from inside the suspected contaminated area.

"Georgiana Reed here," she answered.

"This is Al, George. We have a problem. Joey Caruso, the maintenance guy who found the canister. He's down. Sick and vomiting. Unconscious. We need the medical team to come in and get him."

The medevac helicopter was waiting on a nearby rooftop. George called for transport.

George said, "Crap, this is going to get bad."

The squad went into action, biohazard gear in place, carrying the portable stretcher down the stairway to the subway office. All precautions had been taken as they brought Joey out, in an isolation hood, and loaded him carefully into the unmarked van, which would take him to the heliport.

Inside the office, Marty and the others had watched as Joey was put on an IV drip and oxygen, covered with a protective hood, and then carried out. They were silent, watching this scary scene, all aware that they could be next, wondering if they too had been exposed to a dangerous poison or God knows what.

After Joey was gone, the FBI forensics team took samples and placed them in secure evidence bags. Duplicate samples were secured for the CDC. The hazmat crew thoroughly cleaned the carpet and sofa where Joey had been sitting. The team leader spoke quietly to Marty, asking for Joey's personal information and then left to follow up the transfer of Joey to the ambulance. Marty, the two police officers, and the other guys were still in shock.

Then Marty spoke, knowing his job was to rally his men and get everyone to shake this off and think rationally, especially since they had no idea what caused Joey to suddenly get so sick.

"Okay, guys, lighten up. Joey probably has the flu or something, and that's all. We will find out soon enough what's up, and then we can get back to business as usual. He is probably just hung over."

Some of the guys laughed, which lowered the tension level a little.

Marty continued, "In the meantime, we should enjoy the peace and quiet, relax, and watch some TV or play cards, or something. Right?"

Marty appeared to be upbeat, and the guys began to relax a little. Deep inside, Marty wasn't sure, but until they knew what was what, he saw no need to overreact. Marty had to call Donna, though. He would downplay what happened, saying Joey felt queasy, and they were taking him to the doctor, just to be sure. He didn't know exactly where Joey was being treated, so he didn't have to lie. Donna would have to stay home with the baby anyway. Marty didn't want to think the worst but he was scared.

# 21

Outside, George was on her cell, talking to the three-man team that was transporting Joey. His symptoms were acute, and he needed prompt medical attention. They decided to take him to a secure specialized facility, not risking others if he was infected with some toxic strain or weaponized bio-agent. George agreed. They would take him to the Edgewood Medical Facility. The doctors there had the capability to diagnose and treat him, in case this was some biological infectious disease or toxin. If he had a previously undiagnosed medical problem, no harm done. The decision had been made. They could keep him stable in transit. They hoped.

George then called FBI Field Office Director Fran Jacobs, explaining the status, and Fran said, "Guess we have to wait on the lab report regarding the canister."

Both agreed that no further press releases would be given until they knew more.

George said, "I have a call in to Homeland Security Regional Director Bennett, Fran."

"Good job, George. Let me know immediately if you learn anything."

"Will do."

The New York City Regional Homeland Security Director Bennett called back right away, asking George, "What about the New York Metropolitan Transit Authority? Have you spoken with the department head, Hutchinson—I think his name is—regarding any other possible benign event, perhaps a contamination of some type, a spill, or something accidental that occurred on the platform? Was there an electrical fire, causing smoke, or any other pertinent finding?"

"I spoke to Hutchinson. He has been on the scene most of the morning. Nothing has been found of any causal nature occurring on any of NYC public transportation sites, including the subway system. We are ruling out as many scenarios as possible," answered Reed. She paused.

"Sir, I have an idea. May I get back to you shortly?" she requested.

"Certainly, Ms. Reed. I'm on my way to the Mayor's office. You can reach me on my cell. But I think you would agree that we must move quickly on this."

"Yes, understood."

"Agent Reed, as part of the Counterterrorism Task Force, we want you and your partner, Agent Strickland, to meet us at City Hall, in the Mayor's office at noon. Various department heads will be present to coordinate all efforts."

"Yes, sir, and I believe we will have some information at that time, which could be very helpful to this investigation."

After hanging up, George turned to Mark and said, "Let's try to reach Wally Weber."

Mark looked puzzled momentarily and then smiled.

"Great idea, George." She began to dial the FBI headquarters at Quantico. The operator answered, and George, after giving her special clearance code, asked to speak to Agent Walt Weber.

"One moment, please." The operator returned and said, "I'll patch you through."

"Thanks, "said George, and hung on.

It took a few minutes, but then he picked up, "Weber here." His voice was loud and gravelly. The sound of gunfire could be heard in the background.

# 22

"Georgiana Reed here. Sounds like you're at the range."

"Yes, Agent Reed, getting in some practice," he answered. "What can I do for ya?" he asked.

George replied, "I need your help, and you probably know what we're up against here in New York," she answered.

"Yep, I think I do," he said.

"When can we talk?" she asked.

He said, "Now?"

"Yes, that would be great. Thanks. "

"Fine, give me a few minutes. Let me get back to my office, and I'll call you."

"That would be great," said George."

Wally, with an elbow propped on his desk, patched through. He was about sixty, balding, of average height and a stocky build. He had on a rumpled white shirt, loosened collar and tie, dark slacks, and a Glock 22 in his shoulder holster. He didn't know Georgiana Reed very well but had heard of her. She was considered highly competent and was quite a looker. He had seen her at some FBI functions.

She answered, "Did you get them all in the ten ring?" she asked, smiling.

"Mostly," Wally answered, very low key.

After George introduced Mark on speaker phone, she said, "I would guess you know why I am calling."

He knew what they wanted but would let them lead the way, remaining silent.

"You were in charge of the investigation in '08 that resulted in finding the alleged anthrax perp," George stated. "As I recall, twenty-two were infected, five died. Correct?"

"Yeah, as we were closing in, the bastard offed himself. Pissed me off, big time."

George continued, "You deserved all the credit for tracking that guy down."

Wally said, dismissively, "It was a team effort." He spoke modestly, but they knew he was responsible for finding the killer.

"We could use your expertise on the case we're working now." Wally let her continue, but he had heard plenty about the case from others in the agency.

"It's the possible terrorist attack, in the subway, a potential poison or biological agent," said George.

They briefed him on what they knew, including the telephoned threat, the number of possible victims, and the suspected object in question that had been found on the platform. He asked further questions, and they filled him in.

"Where is the canister now?" he asked.

Mark spoke this time, "Quantico."

Wally said, "You need to know the source of the canister. Then identify the agent and motive, simple as that." He was matter of fact.

"Right," said Georgiana with a chuckle. "What else?"

"The working profile would be this," Wally said. "Look for a scientist, someone inside, with access to toxins, biologic or otherwise, possible ties to a jihadist group. Maybe an ax to grind or psycho. Maybe a combo." Wally leaned back in his squeaky wooden desk chair.

"Other thoughts?"

"Places like Detrick or other centers for chemical and biological warfare are locations to investigate. To jump to a conclusion, take a shot at Edgewood, the ECBC in Maryland. There are other military CBW centers that need to be checked out, as well. You could send investigative teams to the other centers, and you guys can start at Edgewood. They store a lot of bad shit there."

"I think you sized it up for us, Wally. Can you be in on this thing? We could use your help."

"Glad to, Agent Reed."

She said, "Call me George. How about we call you after we check some things out at Edgewood?"

"Sounds good," said Wally. "That will give me time to get some things in place."

"Wally, you know some agents that are experienced in this type of investigation. Can you call them and get the investigative process going at several other locations?"

"Can do, but you know the protocol."

"Yes, I'll call Jacobs, fill her in, then we'll leave for Edgewood."

George called Fran Jacobs and explained how she was going to proceed. Jacobs said to use all agents necessary to look into the various CBW centers. George was advised to contact Director Bennett to arrange security clearance at the APG lab.

George called Bennett to let him know the plan, explaining that Director Jacobs had given full approval, and they would need security clearance at Edgewood.

Bennett said, "You are going there now? What about the meeting?"

George said, "We need to act on some information critical to the investigation. Can you conference us in, sir? We will be in the car for the next two hours."

"Are you sure this is absolutely necessary right now? We want all members of the task force present," he demanded.

"Sir, we would not ask this if it were not crucial to the investigation. One of the Quantico-based agents, Wally Weber, has given us some leads that we must follow up on now. Weber will be checking with you for clearance at other CBW centers, as well. Can that be arranged? We will contact you with any additional information, sir."

"Yes, I'll get whatever clearance you need, but I expect a full report. We should have the meeting pulled together around noon. We will call you." He hung up.

"Fucking bureaucrat," she muttered under her breath.

Then to Mark, she said, "What does the GPS say about the drive time to Edgewood?"

He said, "Not long. It is ninety-five miles, but we have to factor in traffic." He had the red bubble on top, flashing, as he began the route. He grabbed his cell phone, spoke briefly, and then said, "Thanks."

After the call, Mark said, "Our state police escort is going to meet us on I-95."

George knew this was going to be a fun ride and smiled, as she tightened her seat belt.

# 23

"What is it, Frank?" Dave asked.

Dr. Edwards proceeded, saying, "Within the last half hour, we've had three patients brought in, all with flu-like symptoms, most unconscious or nearly so. Standard treatment has been administered, blood drawn, IV fluids, and each seems to have one thing in common. They all used the Express Subway Station this morning. I have moved them to isolation, in case they have been exposed to some type of chemical or biological agent that could put us all in an at-risk emergency situation."

Dave asked, "Have you notified the hospital administrator about this?"

Frank responded, "Yes, and Jim Lucas is informing the FBI, the CDC, Homeland Security, and the NYPD. We are under disaster response conditions, and extra staff have been called in, including three ER physicians. The isolation unit is capable of handling thirty patients, so we are prepared, for the moment."

Thoughts were racing as Dave considered what he had just heard. At this point, they knew nothing.

"Call me when you get lab results."

"Will do," said Edwards, and he hung up.

Chris asked, "What is it, Dave?" He explained, and they discussed possible scenarios.

Dave grabbed the remote off the desk and turned on the TV, sitting on the console on the opposite side of the room. He found the local news channel, which was reporting the latest on the subway shutdown. There had been no further developments, but one eyewitness at the scene saw someone being carried out of the subway station where a suspicious object was rumored to have been found. No press releases or statements were being made at this time. Mayor Donnelly had urged all New Yorkers to remain calm since nothing of significance had been discovered. Traffic was slow but not impossible, since buses and taxis were available. The Mayor requested that everyone remain at home, if possible, to ease the traffic flow in case emergency vehicles needed roadway access.

Dave said, "Check with the nurses' stations and get an update. It could get ugly very fast."

Chris called the nurses' station in the ER.

"Hi, Connie, how is it out there?" asked Chris, trying to keep a lighthearted tone.

"Things are going pretty well, but we could be bombarded with more patients at any moment. It is an unpredictable situation."

"Call me if you need some help," responded Chris. "I'll check on the nurses' lounge and make certain we have food supplies and coffee."

Connie was glad Chris and Dr. Grant were still in the hospital.

Chris gave Dave a warm kiss, touching his face gently, and said, "I better check on supplies, then freshen up a bit."

There was a shower room with lockers next to the nurses' lounge. Fresh scrubs were available, and the nurses had learned to keep extra clothing and personal items at the hospital, in case they had to work double shifts or had gotten soiled handling ill patients.

After starting the coffee, Chris took a shower, dressed in fresh pink scrubs, and ran a comb through her hair. After a touch of coral lipstick and some blush, she looked presentable and headed out to the nursing station. Triage was starting to get busy, and in a few minutes, several ambulances would be arriving with four patients, all with severe flu-like symptoms. Chris called Dave and gave him the information, and he rallied himself for what was ahead.

Dave called Frank, in isolation, and asked about the lab results.

"It looks bad, Dave. Never saw this before, but it's possible that it could be some kind of virus, to act so fast. We are double-checking the results. We sent samples to the lab that the CDC maintains at the pharmaceutical research facility in north Jersey. They are working to get a firm identification. As soon as they have anything, they will call us. The FBI lab at Quantico is working on the ID as well."

Dave said, "You stay in the isolation unit. I assume you are wearing protective clothing, mask, etc. You have nursing staff with you, correct?"

Frank replied, "Three nurses, all fully covered."

"Stay there. No one leaves or enters, and if you need something, we will run it in for you through the locked safe decontamination area."

"Fine with me, so far. We are keeping them stable, hydrated, and are all being treated with the standard anti-viral medications and antibiotics, but one of the older men has some shaky vital signs."

Dave hated to tell him but continued, "Frank, we have four more heading in with the same symptoms. They will be coming your way. I'll get you an extra nurse when I can. We need to send any further patients with these symptoms to another facility, perhaps Edgewood Medical Facility. We can't risk our staff and other patients if this is some virulent strain or bacterial attack of some kind."

"What the fuck are you saying, Dave?" Frank asked.

Dave's voice tightened. "You know exactly what I am saying, Frank. This could turn into a CF, big time," and he hung up.

Dave began dialing the hospital administrator, Jim Lucas, and explained the status. "The CDC has lab samples. Maybe you should call the CDC director. The FBI must be notified, as well. We should divert any further patients with these symptoms to Edgewood Medical Facility and possibly transfer the current patients, soon to be seven, to Edgewood, as well. Call them and explain what we have going on. Got it.?" Dave wasted no words.

"What about the Mayor?" asked Jim.

Dave barked, "I don't give a shit about the Mayor. He is last on my list. Let's get these patients out of here, fucking Stat!"

Dave wondered how many had been infected already.

# 24

Since they had met in January, every weekend was filled, day and night, with Max. During the week, they were in daily contact. They couldn't get enough of each other. They sometimes had dinner out or would order in. Suzy would prepare special dinners for Max, and they would cook, laugh, and sip wine, savoring each moment they shared. They loved spending each night together, naked.

Some Saturday nights, they would dine out, each choosing a favorite restaurant to surprise the other. One particular weekend in the spring, Max took her to the hotel in Baltimore where they had first met. He had reserved the same suite where they had spent their first night, and he had arranged for a special candlelit dinner to be served by the balcony, overlooking the Inner Harbor. Suzy was surprised when they walked into the hotel and he escorted her to the elevator.

"Max, I thought we were having dinner here," queried Suzy.

"We are, baby." And he smiled at her. Her beauty continued to amaze him, as he studied her upturned face, realizing she was delightfully surprised.

"Max, how lovely this will be. Thank you." She spoke softly.

Max was already excited, just being near her. Both were impatient to get to the suite and enjoy the memories of the night they had met, and make more and more memories.

After entering the beautiful and familiar suite, he took her light wrap and hung it in the closet. She was wearing a stunning sleeveless turquoise blue cocktail dress, with a low-cut V-neck that was angled off center. It was just low enough that he could see the slight mound of one of her breasts. She was erotic and sensual, with a flair for dressing perfectly to showcase her exotic beauty. She wore little jewelry, only the diamond drop earrings. He loved watching her walk to the bar, the form-fitting dress hugging her rounded hips, heightening his desire.

An hors d'oeuvres tray was on the bar, next to the chilled champagne. Max poured the sparkling liquid into their glasses, and they sipped slowly, sampling the delicious caviar and the assorted canapés. They talked about their week, with Max saying he had been assigned a difficult project, but it was going well. Suzy said her lab had been busy, but neither could go into much detail. Discretion was required when discussing their work.

Suzy asked, "When will dinner be served?"

Max said, "We will order when we are ready. I thought you might like to look at the menu."

She knew his thoughts. She set her wine glass down, touched his hand, and gently guided him to the softly lit living room. She pulled him down next to her on the plush sofa, and they began kissing, deep tongue kisses, ravenous kisses, his arms enveloping her. She was hungry for him, her desire and need equal to his. He leaned her backward, sliding his warm strong hand under her dress, feeling her thigh, his hand finding her opening, covered with silk. He slid her panties aside and touched her. She moaned, his lips on hers, their wet kisses full of longing, and she began moving against his fingers. They stopped just long enough for him to remove her dress and panties, and then he started kissing her breasts, so exquisite and her taste was thrilling. She was ready for him instantly, and he took his clothes off, put his knee between her legs, spreading them, opening her body for him alone. She was touching his hardness, meant only for her, and after touching him, holding him close to her body, rubbing him against her wet opening, she guided him into her, his cock filling her.

She wrapped her legs around him, her stiletto heels still on, pulling him deeper into her. His touch, their kisses, their longing, his body completing hers, they made love passionately, moving rhythmically against each other, heart to heart, saying love words, and they both came forcefully, in a huge burst of emotion. His fierce possession of her body was complete. She gave herself fully to him, and he to her, in all ways. Their lovemaking was so powerful, enough seemed never enough.

"I love you, Suzy, and I will always love you," he said, from the depths of his heart and soul.

The tear droplets fell from her eyes. He was still on top of her, kissing her, his arms enveloping her.

"Max, my darling Max, I love you so."

# 25

Max was nestled against Suzy's back, both still naked. He awoke slowly, lightly kissing her shoulders. She stirred, moving back against him, to get closer to his warmth. His body encompassed hers, and she loved the feeling. He loved her small proportions and the feel of her beautiful body against his. He couldn't stop his desire, and she didn't want him to stop. They began to make love, his lips on the back of her neck, his hands on her breasts, as he moved in and out of her slowly, never wanting to stop. It was as though nothing existed in the world but them. She gasped, and he felt her body respond to his, and he came into her, both feeling they were in a dream, the rare moments, their rare magic. They savored each other, falling asleep wrapped tightly together.

A few hours later, Max drove Suzy home, pulling his Mercedes into Suzy's driveway, using the opener that Suzy had given him to raise the garage doors. He parked in the space next to her Lexus. He was comfortable in her world. It had been a beautiful night, and both were glad they had all day Sunday to be together. It was a warm spring day, and they planned on taking a swim in the heated outdoor pool after lunch. Both loved being active and exercising together. Fitness was part of his training, and Suzy had always been disciplined to exercise. It helped keep the gremlins at bay.

Suzy had to shower, change clothes, and do a few obligatory household chores for a short while. She had started coffee before going upstairs. They had stopped for fresh bagels and cream cheese on their way back from the Inner Harbor, and she had oranges for making fresh juice.

Max called to Suzy upstairs, "I need to make a few calls and check my email, Suzy."

Suzy replied, "Sure, Max, use my office."

Max entered the small office off the living room and sat in the plush leather chair behind Suzy's uniquely designed desk. It was made of teak, a Chinese antique and family heirloom. The burgundy Oriental rug covering the hardwood floor, along with the ornate burgundy and green silk lined curtains, added warmth to the décor of the room.

Max began looking for some notepaper and a pen. The center desk drawer seemed stuck, and then realizing it was locked, he searched for a key. It was taped under the bronze desk lamp, as he expected. He smiled. He found a note pad and several pens in a special partition in the front of the drawer. That was all he needed. Then he saw the .38 S&W. He picked it up, opened the cylinder, and saw the Hornady hollow points. He placed it carefully back where he found it. Nice little bauble. My girl is full of surprises, he smiled. He noticed the manila envelope, unmarked, and the two photos. He stared at both, seemingly of the same girl. What a beautiful but very young Chinese girl who looked like a teenage version of Suzy. They were old black-and-white photographs. Maybe it was Suzy. He looked in the envelope. The message was cryptic, typewritten, and contained only five lines:

*4.7: D-Day.*

*10 mil. 842-66895. D + 1.*

*+ L*

*Failure unacceptable.*

*The Organization.*

Max noticed the copier on the credenza. He made copies of the note and photographs, then placed the originals back in the drawer, and stuck the folded copies in his pocket.

# 26

Mike had called the doorman to retrieve his car from the garage. He grabbed his small suitcase, in case he had to spend the night. He knew the drive to Johns Hopkins would take at least three hours plus, on a good day, but he wanted to take the car so he could bring Maggie home comfortably. She could recover from this flu bug at home. It seemed the most practical thing to do.

He threw the bag in the backseat of their Audi and tipped Arnie, the doorman. He mentioned he might be away overnight and to watch for the boys and Annie to get home from school.

Arnie got along great with all of the residents, but he felt close to the Ryans and did many favors for them. He had been doorman at their building for a long time and was well-liked by everyone in the building. Arnie had Mike's cell phone number in case of emergency.

"Is there further news about the subway problem, Arnie?" asked Mike.

"No, Mr. Ryan, but I see lots of traffic and emergency vehicles going by and what looks like yellow police tape around the subway entrance. You might want to turn left and go around the block to avoid that area," he answered.

"Yes, you're right." Mike could see the congestion and some activity surrounding the entrance just a short distance down the street.

Arnie continued, "I thought I saw an ambulance's flashing lights down there, not too long ago, but I don't know what that was all about."

"Crap," thought Mike, that doesn't sound good.

"Thanks, Arnie. I'll let you know what is going on. Wish me luck." He waved at Arnie as he pulled out into traffic.

Mike had the hospital address and programmed it into the GPS. The directions were simple, but he wanted to take the quickest route possible. He turned on the car radio, hoping to hear of any further news of the subway closing. Mike followed the doorman's advice and turned left at the next intersection. Traffic was heavy, as always, but this area was tight. He realized he had a very long drive ahead, but he had to get to Maggie.

As he sat in the heat, almost at a standstill, he listened to the news, and so far, there had been no further information about what had been found in the subway. The announcer did mention that one of the subway workers had gotten sick with flu-like symptoms, but there was no word on his condition. Mike was glad he kept water in the car, grabbed a bottle from the backseat console, and took a large gulp.

"Damn," Mike said, out loud, "just damn." And he hit the steering wheel as his frustrations grew.

Traffic was crawling. He had been on the road for an hour and had made little progress. The radio abruptly drew his attention, and sudden fear hit him.

"We interrupt this program with a breaking news bulletin."

# 27

Flight 227 was about a half hour out of Miami International Airport. The flight had been far from routine, thought John. He and Allen were deeply concerned about Maggie and the safety of his crew and passengers. Allen continued to monitor the latest news about the NYC crisis. The city was on high alert status due to a possible terrorist attack of the subway system. The potential threat had not yet been identified. In press releases, the Mayor had stated that "an object" had been found and was being analyzed by the FBI, but everyone was to remain calm. Nothing substantive had been reported. One city worker had been hospitalized, but the status of his condition was still unknown. Several hospitals had reported a rise in the number of patients requesting treatment in their emergency departments, but this could have been coincidental.

John was uncertain of what was going on, but these thoughts had to be put aside as he went through his pre-landing checklist. He heard the double knock on the door and reached back to unlock it. Terry entered the cockpit.

"Hi, Terry, how is it going back there?" asked John.

"I'm not sure," and she hesitated. "I am feeling queasy, a bit lightheaded, probably nothing serious, but I wanted you to know. I have told the other guys about it, and they are helping me. I need to sit down, so I am heading to the rear of the plane to work on the flight report and rest until we get to Miami. This just hit me suddenly."

She continued, "Mary, Jackie, and Justin can handle the rest of the flight. The food service is complete, and everything is stowed away."

John looked at her closely, noting her paleness and shaky demeanor. She had pulled down the jump seat and sat still, looking washed out.

"I must be coming down with the flu or some weird bug."

John said, "You probably have a virus. Don't worry. Find a seat in the back and we'll have you on the ground soon. I'll radio flight control that we need a sub for the return flight to NYC, and you can check in with Health Services at the airport."

"What's our ETA?" asked Terry, hoping they would get there soon.

"We are almost there, maybe another twenty-five minutes until touch down. The tower will clear us for a quick landing, and we'll have someone meet us at the gate with a wheelchair to pick you up."

Terry was relieved. She thanked the guys and walked to rear of the plane, keeping her composure, not wanting to show any signs that she was feeling wobbly. She sat on the rear jump seat and began working on the flight reports. It was hard for her to concentrate, but she finished the routine paperwork. Her head was throbbing. She hoped she hadn't caught whatever Maggie had, but she knew something was seriously wrong. Her symptoms were just like Maggie's, and they had begun so suddenly.

The seatbelt sign came on as they were making their final approach. Terry was sipping the orange juice that Justin had brought to her. He was sitting next to her, his arm around her, in support. She was grateful to have his help and felt relief when the wheels touched down.

She wasn't aware when they carried her off the plane, and the EMTs placed her in the ambulance to take her to the Miami University Medical Center.

Captain Wesley and First Officer Delaney were still sitting in the cockpit, wondering what the hell was going on.

# 28

Lee had only vague memories from her early childhood, of her weeping mother clinging to her, as she was being dragged away by a man and woman and taken to a large gray building, placed in a cold room with many small beds, filled with other children, many who were crying and alone in large cribs. Lee remembers crying herself to sleep. There were other dark images. The hunger she felt daily, the sour milk, tasteless, cold mush, and if lucky, white sticky rice, served occasionally with hard bread, or her favorite, a small bowl of warm broth.

Lee could no longer remember her mother's face, only a pervasive sadness that crept up now and then, but mostly it was buried so deeply inside that she didn't know or recognize any emotions. Nothing could touch her or hurt her ever. Absence of feeling had become essential to her survival.

She was aware that she had lived in Shanghai since she was a young girl, but she wasn't certain for how long. Her trip from the orphanage in Beijing to this dilapidated hotel in the bustling overcrowded city was a blurred memory. She found out later that she was sold to some men, whose faces she now knew well. They had paid the orphanage and then taken her on a long journey, ending in Shanghai, to this run-down hotel, with other girls like herself, young, pretty, emotionless, where they learned quickly how to survive. They were adept at it. They were also loyal to each other, and she learned from them what was expected of her. She had grown accustomed to strangers touching her, though at first it was mortifying. The older girls told her what to do and how to survive. Now, nothing was forbidden, and she had gotten used to the routine of her stark life.

Lou E and Mick owned the girls, kept them amply provided for, and made sure they were obedient when it came to satisfying the clients. They bought the girls' clothing and makeup, cheap but enticing, and provided them with all their needs, even bringing in a doctor if any became ill. Lee never saw any money; she just lived as the others did, from day to day, resting in the daylight, eating food that was provided, and waiting for the darkness to come to find out what was in store for them. Some of the girls were migrants, who had traveled to the city seeking better paying jobs but ended up doing the only job available. They were all young, barely in their teens, but that was the attraction. Men wanted these nubile exquisitely beautiful toys to pleasure them, and Lou E and Mick took great care of these delightful innocents.

Prostitution was a lucrative business in Shanghai and in many large Chinese cities. Though illegal, the government pretended it didn't exist. The tourist trade flourished, and businessmen like Lou E and Mick added much to the economic growth of the city.

Lee was a favorite because of her delicate, sensual beauty and gentle nature. Mick, and especially Lou E, favored her and had become attached to her. She was fond of them, and as she grew older, they kept her only for the highest paying clients and themselves. At times, she thought of another life, a life she had heard about from the other girls. She had learned to read while at the orphanage and hoped that one day she would be able to experience more than the life in which she was imprisoned. One memory had remained, of a woman with outstretched arms, reaching for her, crying for her, and Lee wanted to see her again. There was another vague memory. She kept seeing an image, but it never clarified. Something was missing. She wanted to know the mysteries of her past life. The feelings of emptiness and loss were nearly unbearable.

# 29

Suzy drove to her parents' house, aware that her dad would be still be at the university. It was around 11:30 a.m., and she needed to speak privately to her mother. The investigation into the morning's "event" had started, and she hoped her absence would go unnoticed, at least for a short while. It had taken her forty-five minutes to get from Edgewood to the prestige suburb of Newark, Delaware, where her parents lived. Suzy could only communicate with her mother in person. She was still exhausted from her sleepless night.

Rose Lin answered the door in chic beige slacks, white tailored blouse, a strand of pearls, and matching earrings. Suzy marveled at her mother's exquisite beauty. She had Asian features, straight black hair, to her shoulders, and a youthful, slender figure. Suzy could see her own reflection in her mother's face.

"Suzy, my beautiful daughter, what a delightful surprise. Please come in." She hugged her daughter close. She held Suzy for a moment and then stepped back to look at her.

Rose Lin smiled and then asked, "Would you care for some tea?" Suzy followed her mother into the comfortable but modern kitchen.

"No thank you, mother, but please go ahead. No students today?" asked Suzy, grabbing a bottle of water from the refrigerator. She sat on one of the white French provincial style bar stools at the granite-topped center island.

"Several students cancelled, so I am free for the rest of the day."

Suzy was glad and knew her father wouldn't be home until dinnertime. He was completing the final paperwork due at the end of each semester. They would be free to speak. Suzy looked around at the warm kitchen, thinking of the happy memories she enjoyed, growing up in such a wonderful loving home with adoring parents. She loved the small circular glass kitchen table that fit perfectly in the nook of the bay window, where she and her parents had eaten most of their meals. It overlooked the beautiful garden, full of colorful flowers, already in full bloom. Suzy felt fortunate to have grown up in such a beautiful home with her two loving parents.

"How is Father?" asked Suzy.

He was ten years older than her mother, and Suzy was concerned about his health. It had been recently discovered that he had heart arrhythmia problems. He was under doctor's care, on medication, and also had pacemaker. He was stable, but Suzy worried about him.

Her mother reassured Suzy, "He is doing just fine, my dear. No worries."

"Does he have classes during the summer quarter?" asked Suzy.

"Yes, just two," said Rose Lin, "but he feels well, and keeping busy helps maintain his positive attitude. As you know, that is the secret to health, happiness, and long life." She smiled.

"Tell me about you, Suzy. I can see in your face that you are burdened." Rose Lin studied her daughter's face carefully. "I have heard about New York City and the terrorist attack. Are you involved in the investigation? I heard that they found something in the subway."

Her mother knew that Suzy couldn't talk about work, but Rose Lin was concerned for her daughter's safety. She was also worried about the terrorist threat and what it could mean on a large scale.

"Mother, I need to tell you something, but it could have dire consequences. I must have your word of honor that you will not disclose this information to anyone, only Father," said Suzy.

Her solemn tone frightened Rose Lin. Suzy couldn't believe she had to talk about this, but it was crucial, since it directly involved her mother.

"My daughter, you know that I am here for you and will help in any way that I can," answered her mother. "What is it? Is something wrong?" Her mother's voice was plaintive.

"I know about Lee," Suzy stated, placing an envelope in her mother's hands.

Her mother's delicate face froze. Rose Lin spoke no words, but a single glistening teardrop began flowing down her angular, beautifully sculpted cheekbone.

# 30

A s Dave sat in Jim Lucas's office, he spoke on the phone with the CDC director, Dr. Ambrose. The test results of the canister were as yet undetermined, but the patients' symptoms suggested a virus of unknown origin. The CDC lab in north Jersey was still working on the lab samples, as well. Additional nasal and throat swabs along with blood samples were on their way to the CDC lab in Atlanta. The symptoms of the patients, all of whom had been in the subway station where the "object in question" had been found, were all similar: coughing, breathing difficulties, severe headaches, fever, nausea, chills, weakness, muscle aches, and sore throat. Some were affected more severely than others.

Dave and Dr. Ambrose were deep in conversation, when Jim got a phone call from Dr. Edwards in the isolation unit.

"What is it, Frank?" asked Jim.

"One of our patients, an older gentleman who came in earlier today, just died from respiratory failure. His wife has been told, and we have the hospital chaplain with her now. He was in the subway station this morning."

"Holy shit," said Jim.

Dr. Edwards continued, "He had a history of chronic bronchitis and emphysema. He was vulnerable to any severe respiratory infection."

"How are the other patients doing?" asked Jim.

"Not good. They are all coughing and have multiple acute symptoms. We are trying various anti-viral medications. Without knowing the strain, we don' know which medication will be most effective. It is too soon to tell." Frank was matter of fact.

"Keep me posted, and you and your staff use extreme caution. We don't have an f-ing clue what we have on our hands." Jim was concerned.

"We are, but thanks, Jim, we appreciate that. I just wish we knew what we are dealing with."

Dave was saying to Dr. Ambrose, "Until we know for sure, we continue to treat and contain."

Dr. Ambrose agreed that they would stay in touch as more information was obtained.

After a few more minutes of conversation, they concluded the meeting.

Dave asked Jim, "What?"

Jim was ashen. "We lost one of the patients in isolation. The older man, John Keaton. He had a history of emphysema and chronic bronchitis. Respiratory failure."

"Damn!" Dave sat for a few moments and then said, "I need to check on something."

After reaching his office, Dave logged on to the *New England Journal of Medicine* and began a search for viral information. An article about avian flu captured his interest. It was an unlikely source, but many symptoms matched those of the patients that they were currently treating. Could this be possible, he wondered?

It is rare and is transmitted from wild birds to domesticated birds, like turkeys, chickens, and ducks, and then to humans, if eaten. Pandemic risk can follow. As he read further, the more suspicious he became. When bird flu affects humans, it is often deadly. Then again, it could be a swine influenza, which has many similarities to avian flu, but is transferred, human to human. That would make more sense.

He enlarged the search criteria to include the common symptoms that had been presented, including quick onset and respiratory distress. The results suggested other possibilities including West Nile virus or the norovirus, sometimes called the cruise ship virus. Both could be deadly and fast spreading. He couldn't rule out chemical inhalation or pneumonia, either.

He punched Jim's extension. "Hey, Jim, I don't know what the hell we are dealing with. I found information that points to anything from West Nile to avian flu, chemical contact or coincidence. Whatever it is, we're fucked. At this point, it doesn't matter anyway."

Jim said, "You're right. We are fucked. And wait till you hear this. I just heard a news report that a Century Air flight, departing from LaGuardia this morning, made an emergency landing in Baltimore, approximately one-half hour into the flight. A flight attendant was transported to Johns Hopkins. She had severe flu-like symptoms, and I guess she was pretty much out of it."

"I wonder if she was on the subway platform this morning."

Jim hesitated. "Yes."

"Fucking A…" Dave said.

# 31

Dave went back to his office, and closed the door. He texted Chris. "My office. D"

It only took a few minutes for Chris to get there. She looked beautiful, even in her hospital scrubs. He had showered in the doctors' lounge and was dressed in his standard ER attire of jeans, running shoes, dress shirt with sleeves rolled up, and tie. She closed the door, and they embraced. They kissed softly, and then passionately, with desire. He was pulling her as close to him as possible.

"I love you so much, Chris," Dave said.

"I love you, sweetheart, so very much," she responded, feeling secure in his arms. "What is this, Dave? What is going on?" asked Chris, knowing this was serious. She saw the concern in his eyes.

He took her face in his hands and spoke firmly, "I want you to go home now. Things are going in a direction I don't like, and until we have answers, I want you out of here." Fearing for her safety, he wanted her out of the hospital.

Chris said, "I heard about the man dying in isolation, but he had pre-existing health issues and was at high risk."

"True enough, but allow me to be cautious. You are tired. You need to go home, and don't come back to work until I know what is going on." Dave was firm. He was scared, not just for her, but the entire hospital and staff.

"I don't want to leave you, Dave, please." She never wanted to be anywhere but with him.

He ignored her. "What is the status in the ER now?"

Chris said, "Things are stable but busy. The subway is still shut down. The Center City Hospital administrator called Jim Lucas. They have received several patients with flu-like symptoms. The military is helping transport them to Edgewood. It is precautionary. The patients just happened to be on the subway platform in question, so they don't want to place any hospitals in jeopardy."

Dave spoke quietly "I am concerned, Chris. I have some hunches, but we need lab confirmations."

"What do you think it is, Dave?" she queried.

"I'm not sure, but my guess is a dangerous airborne virus of unknown origin, possibly mutated, as indicated by the uncommonly short incubation period. The CDC or the FBI will give us the answers we need, though we can only treat with certain antiviral medications, no matter what it is, and they are limited in quantity."

Chris said, "I think I should stay. I can rest here if necessary, and the other staff nurses will need breaks. Our ER is busy, under routine circumstances." She was right, but he didn't want her exposed to this unknown virus. He loved her dedication to her job, patients, and coworkers, but he also knew she needed to be near him. He needed her also, but protecting her was foremost.

"Okay, Chris, stay, for now," he said. He held her, not wanting to let go.

"Did Vicki call? How is Carolyn?" asked Chris.

"Thank God, Carolyn is home. Vicki is very upset. I told her I had to stay here and asked her to stay home and not let Carolyn go out. I think she will do as I asked," Dave said.

When it came to their daughter, fortunately Vicki was a good mother. That was all he could ask of her.

# 32

Max walked into the remote CIA office, one of many maintained in the DC area. His friend of over twenty years, Greg Hammond, worked for the NCS, the National Clandestine Service, which is the secret investigative arm of the CIA. Greg and Max had graduated from West Point in the same class, and after Greg finished his tour of duty, he was recruited to work for the CIA, the non-military intelligence gathering agency.

"Max, it's good to see you," greeted Greg, giving Max a warm handshake. "It's been too long."

Greg's office was sparsely furnished and soundproof. There were venetian blinds on one window, plain beige walls, and light brown carpet. There was a comfortable leather desk chair and a large oak desk with a brass desk lamp, a laptop, telephone, and a yellow legal pad and pen. A metal filing cabinet was in one corner.

"What can I get you?" He reached for the phone to buzz his assistant for some coffee.

"Nothing, thanks, Greg, but you go ahead."

"I'm fine, too," Greg said. "It's been a long time. What have you been up to? I heard you're working for the Joint Chiefs. Pretty nice gig, with some perks, no doubt." He smiled.

Max laughed. "It's a great gig. You know how it is. Professional ass kisser mostly, but sometimes I actually get asked my opinion." Both men laughed, knowing they were in the business of keeping secrets.

"You look great," stated Greg. "Keeping in shape, I see."

"You, too. It must be the academy thing." They were similar, instilled with self- discipline and strict core values. Both were glad to see each other again.

"You ever get married, Greg? I remember that little brunette you were dating, the one with the impressive figure."

Greg said, "No, I thought she was serious, but I just couldn't spend enough time with her, and I guess she found a nine to fiver to keep her happy." He laughed, but Max sensed it was halfhearted.

"What about you, Max? You had them lined up," he smiled.

Everyone was aware of Max's looks and magnetic charm, even the guys, but Max was the only one who didn't catch on. He had been career oriented and not much for serious dating. That is, until now.

"Actually, no, I am not married, but that could change, even at my age. Forty-two. Damn, that sounds old."

"I hear you," said Greg. "So you have one on the line?" he asked, raised his eyebrows.

"Yes, and frankly, that is why I am here." Greg leaned forward, giving Max a questioning smirk.

"What gives?" Greg knew there was more to this meeting than old friends catching up.

"I need a favor," asked Max.

"You got it." Greg leaned back in his leather chair.

Max pulled an envelope from his briefcase and slid it across the desk. Greg opened it and read the brief message several times. He studied the photographs, memorizing both.

"I need to know what these mean. I want to know their connection to the lady I am seeing, Dr. Suzy Chen, assistant director of Edgewood Labs at the APG." He filled Greg in on all that he knew about Suzy's background and how he had obtained the information.

"I'm impressed. So how serious are you about this lady?" asked Greg, looking Max in the eyes.

"Very."

Greg understood. "When do you need to know?"

"As soon as possible." Max spoke emphatically. Greg knew this was not just ordinary curiosity.

"You came to the right place," answered Greg.

"Thanks, Greg. I mean it," said Max.

"This must be some lady." Greg smiled.

"You can't fucking imagine," Max said, shaking his head. "I may be in over my head."

# 33

The CDC in Atlanta was getting updated reports from several NYC hospitals that there were significant numbers of patient arrivals, presenting with severe flu-like symptoms. The emergency departments were doing their best to stabilize these patients, keep them isolated, and treat them with anti-viral medications and antibiotics. Dr. Ambrose was notified of these cases since most seemed, in some way, to be connected to the Express Subway platform. Concern was mounting that this was atypical of a normal flu outbreak. The spread was rapid, and the severity and onset of the symptoms were extraordinary.

Dr. Ambrose contacted the research lab in Jersey. They were working on the samples from the various patients stricken with the unknown virus. So far, they had nothing to report. He knew the FBI lab was looking at the canister and its possible connection to the virus in question. He was hoping that the canister would answer some of their questions and even perhaps diminish their concerns. Additional samples would be arriving in Atlanta later in the day.

So far, there had been no definitive identification of the presumed virus. The CDC was tracking the outbreak. This virus had, no doubt, affected many who had had gone home and exposed their families. Some had gone to work, exposing coworkers, or many had left the city via plane or automobile, taking the virus with them. He heard on the news about an airliner making an emergency landing in Baltimore with a sick crew member. He wondered if there might be a connection. As he was thinking of the ramifications, there was a quiet knock on his office door. It was Amy, his assistant. "Dr. Ambrose, Mayor Donnelly of New York City is on line one." Thanking her, he picked up the phone.

"Dr. Ambrose speaking."

"One moment please," said the operator. After a few minutes, the Mayor came on the line.

"This is Mayor Donnelly speaking. Is this Dr. Ambrose?" he asked.

"Yes, this is Ambrose."

Donnelly, not hesitating, said, "We need your help, Dr. Ambrose. First of all, do you have anything to report regarding the subway incident samples?"

"No, sir. We hope to know something soon," Ambrose answered. "Our lab in New Jersey will let me know as soon as they have an identification. More samples will be studied here. We are waiting for their delivery." He looked at his watch, noting it was 11:00 a.m. "These identifications can take time. And no reports from Quantico, as yet."

"The regional director of Homeland Security, Tom Bennett, has called a meeting for noon today in my office. Could you possibly conference in? There will be representatives present from various agencies, including the police commissioner, Health and Human Services, FEMA, the NYC Metropolitan Transit Authority, and the FBI, including two agents working on the case. The Deputy Mayor, Mary Henderson, will be attending, as well. We need your input, Dr. Ambrose."

"Yes, of course. Let's go over some agenda items," answered Dr. Ambrose.

The Mayor said, "Fine, thank you. Our assistants will sort out the conference call." They continued their discussion, with Ambrose jotting down critical points. He would be prepared and hoped to have some test results.

Ambrose called his assistant, Amy, into his office. "The Mayor's assistant is on the phone. Please arrange the conference call that will connect me to the noon meeting."

Amy nodded, "Yes, sir," and returned to her office.

Ambrose dialed extension twelve.

"Paul Miller speaking." Miller was the logistics and distribution manager for emergency supplies.

"Paul, Ambrose here. We may need large quantities of antiviral medications. Please inventory what is available and their locations. The epicenter of the possible outbreak is New York. I need to know what we have and how soon we can transport these supplies. Please call me back as soon as possible."

"Yes, I'll see what quantities are available." Paul knew what this meant. He had heard the news reports coming out of New York. Nothing had been substantiated but he suspected the worst.

"This is classified," Ambrose said and then added, "Please get back to me as soon as possible."

"Yes, sir," answered Paul.

"One more thing, Paul. Please alert Dr. Rudolph. As soon as we ID the virus, we will begin the manufacture of a vaccine. Rudy needs a heads-up on this," said Ambrose. "We need his team ready by this afternoon. We will need all drug companies' cooperation in this effort, as well. Please notify those on our list of approved manufacturers to be on standby."

"Yes, Dr. Ambrose, I'll call Rudy first."

"Thanks," said Ambrose.

His next call was to the tracking center. The CDC was getting reports indicating numerous patients with severe influenza-like symptoms were being admitted to medical facilities in various parts of the country, but the majority of cases were in the New York and New Jersey area. He would have updated counts and locations for the noon meeting.

Dr. Ambrose put his head in his hands. He thought of the months it would take to manufacture a safe and effective vaccine, with all the phases and trials necessary. He could only imagine how many would be dead by then.

# 34

uzy drove back to her office as quickly as she could. She didn't want to attract attention to her lengthy absence. The lab director, Dr. Eric Adams, was out of the office for the afternoon, something to do with "moving his college age son back home from the university," code known around the office that he was meeting Karen from Human Resources for a "noon-er." His car was still gone from the parking lot, so she knew that he wouldn't be aware of her extended absence. His mind would be "distracted" anyway. "What a pig," she thought. It was the perfect time to implement the next step of her assignment.

His office wasn't far from hers. Most staffers were busy, and it wasn't unusual for Suzy to be in and out of Dr. Adams's office, sometimes several times each day. She walked down the empty carpeted hallway and, with a quick look, opened his unlocked office door and stepped inside, locking the door behind her. It was a well-appointed office and richly decorated, befitting his title, which, if life had at all been fair, should have been hers. Dr. Adams had made sure that she, the "Chink broad," wouldn't get the promotion.

What a prick. He was attractive, and she had dated him steadily for several months. He was Mr. Suave, and she fell for it. Damn, how could she ever have ever fallen for him. She had believed his every word and thought he truly loved her. He had promised her further advancements, how they would work together on fascinating life-saving discoveries, never seeing or believing, or wanting to believe, who he truly was. How abruptly she had found out the truth.

Suzy put hostility aside for the moment, needing full concentration, and stepped behind his desk. She opened the laptop, which was sitting on a small computer stand, just to the right of his desk. She was well acquainted with his habits, after many months of observation, and knew he always left his computer behind during his trysts. After accessing the network, Suzy logged on to the secret e-mail account she had set up from his laptop. She wrote a new e-mail, with the brief, memorized message, and saved it as a "draft" making it appear to be a "dead drop."

All of this took only a few minutes. She shut down the computer, wiped the keys with the handkerchief she had placed in her lab coat pocket, closed the laptop, and wiped off the lid. She turned the light off in his office. His tall oak bookcase was against the wall on the left side of his desk. She grabbed a book from the shelf, *The Study of Virology*, a reference she frequently borrowed. As Suzy opened the door, she glanced around to make sure no one was in the hall. Suzy walked down the hall to the coffee room, carrying the book. She poured some hot water for tea, grabbed a teabag, and walked back to her office, waved hello to her assistant, Beth, who was talking on the phone in the office adjacent to Suzy's.

"That went well," she thought. "Bastard!" she said under her breath.

# 35

George and Mark were headed to ECBC, the Edgewood Chemical and Biological Center. They wanted to speak to Dr. Adams, the lab director as soon as possible, regarding the possible toxin or agent in question. They needed to know who had access to the delivery, storage, and testing of the dangerous biological agents and toxins. The more information they could obtain, the sooner the perpetrator or perpetrators would be found.

The drive had started out slowly. George was making notes as Mark made his way through the city. He placed the red flashing light on top of his car to ease the way through traffic snarls. He got to I-95, hooked up with the state police car, and headed south. Traffic was steady, and they were making good time. The siren helped.

Occasionally, George would glance over at Mark and study his face and strong forearms as he drove. He was intense, and she could tell he was thinking about the case. He was going over the evidence and trying to piece things together, but this particular event was of vast magnitude, with consequences difficult to comprehend. They were both determined to find the person or persons responsible.

Mark followed the Maryland State Police escort to the secure entrance of the Edgewood Lab. Mark gave a wave of thanks to the trooper who responded with a nod as he pulled away. Two well-armed MPs flanked the twelve-foot high wrought iron gates in front of the Edgewood complex. One of the guards approached the car and asked Mark for ID.

After looking it over, he said, "Wait here, sir." He went into the security booth, spoke on his radio, and then approached Mark's car again.

"Agent Strickland, your escort will be with you any moment. May I see your ID, ma'am?" he asked. George passed it to him, and after looking it over, he handed it back, saying, "Thanks."

"Please open your trunk, sir." Mark pushed the release on the dashboard.

The guard stepped to the rear of the car and, a moment later, shut the trunk. He returned to the booth and opened the gate. A staff car was waiting inside, and Mark followed the car to the Security Administration Building. He pulled into the space alongside the staff car, and Lieutenant Randall, wearing her dress blues, got out, introduced herself to Mark and George, and requested that they follow her. They were shown into a small lobby of drab military décor and signed in at the desk. Lieutenant Randall said she would be their escort and gave them some background on the Edgewood Laboratory.

George and Mark followed Randall as she drove to the main lab offices, not far from where they were. Lt. Randall parked in front of the building, and after Mark parked the Mustang, Randall led them through double glass doors into the reception area. The lieutenant stepped aside as George showed her ID to the receptionist and asked to speak with Dr. Adams. The receptionist said that Dr. Adams was out at the moment, but he should be return shortly if they wanted to wait.

"Yes, we'll wait," said George, with some irritation. George noticed the armed military guards standing at attention near the entrance. The Edgewood lab had a high level of security presence, understandably so. The receptionist, Stacy, offered them coffee or a cool beverage, and both opted for the second.

"What time does Dr. Adams normally return from lunch?" asked Georgiana, as she was handed the tall glass of iced tea.

"It varies," said Stacy. "I think he had an errand today, so he might be late."

George continued, "Is there anyone else we could speak with regarding your facility's procedures and functions?"

Stacy said, "Dr. Chen is the assistant director. Perhaps she is here and could speak to you, if that would be helpful."

"Yes, please," Georgiana said.

From Georgiana's experience, assistants often shared more information, having less at stake.

Stacy said, "She just got back from lunch. Let me check."

After a few minutes, Stacy hung up her phone and said, "Dr. Chen will be with you shortly."

"Thanks very much," said George.

While waiting for Dr. Chen, Mark and George went over their list of questions. Lieutenant Randall was staying close by, but out of hearing range. George asked Mark how they should start the interview.

He kept his voice low, saying, "Let's start by asking if she has heard of the patient admitted to the Edgewood Medical facility. We can go from there." George nodded in agreement.

Stacy ushered them to the conference room, not far from the reception area. Randall followed but stood outside the doorway.

LINDA WELLS

The conference room was well furnished, with a lamp table, telephone, a tall fluted corner lamp, and a large conference table, with seating for twelve. A large framed aerial photograph of the APG was hanging on one wall.

"Please have a seat. It should only be a few minutes."

When Stacy returned, accompanied by Dr. Chen, she made introductions, asked if they cared for more refreshments, and then left, closing the door behind her.

George and Mark were caught off guard by Dr. Chen's beauty and elegant appearance. Mark was clearly intrigued by her knockout good looks. The white lab coat over Dr. Chen's black linen sheath dress couldn't hide her spectacular figure. The spiked open-toed black patent leather heels revealed turquoise nail polish. The shoes highlighted her sexy legs, as well. But her tone was serious, and she seemed somewhat stand offish. But why not? It isn't often that the FBI would want an interview, but from the morning's news reports, she should have expected an investigation.

They stood and shook her hand. "It is a pleasure meeting you. Thank you for seeing us on such short notice," said George.

"Please have a seat." Suzy motioned toward the chairs as she sat at the head of the table, closest to the door. Dr. Chen then asked, "How can I be of assistance, Agent Reilly and Agent Strickland?"

"I guess you've heard of the recent admission to the medical facility here at the Proving Grounds of the New York City subway maintenance worker with a possible exposure to a poisonous toxin or biological agent?" asked Mark.

"Yes, of course," she said. "He is in serious condition." She paused. "At this time, our chemists are working on the specimens. We expect a preliminary analysis soon."

Georgiana said, "We have reason to believe that there was a terrorist attack at an Express Subway Station, with one worker in question, and possibly others, exposed to a toxin or possible weapons grade agent of an unknown nature. Our agency received a possible warning that such an attack would take place. Evidence found at the scene, currently at the Quantico lab, leads us to conclude that this is, in fact, the most probable scenario." George spoke firmly. "Due to the seriousness of what we are dealing with, we must be frank."

"Certainly," said Dr. Chen, her blank facial expression unchanged, but Mark noticed light moisture forming above her upper lip.

Suzy said, "Perhaps you should discuss this with Dr. Adams. He will return from lunch soon."

Mark was staring at her and said, "We would like to speak with him when he returns. In the meantime, give us some background on what goes on here at Edgewood, and if there is any likelihood that a toxic agent could have been stolen from this facility and used in such an attack?" He waited.

Dr. Chen was adamant. "Absolutely not. No materials of such dangerous nature have been removed from our secure containment center. We are a military facility and a leading research campus. Our renowned staff have impeccable reputations. There has been no breech in our security. Our chemists, along with those from the CDC are currently working jointly on specimens possibly relating to the 'incident' in New York City. As soon as we have information, we will notify Dr. Ambrose and Homeland Security Director Bennett, as has been requested."

She stood up. "Now, if you have any further questions, I suggest you speak to Dr. Adams or check with the CDC."

Mark and George stood, realizing that this meeting had just come to a screeching halt.

"Thank you, Dr. Chen," George said.

Chen said, dismissively, "I must check on the progress of the testing. Please excuse me."

Mark's eyes followed her as she walked out.

George looked at Mark and said, "I guess the meeting is over."

George said, "Find out everything you can about Chen."

Mark nodded agreement, but something wasn't right with this chick.

As Suzy walked back to her office, Beth intercepted her. "The lab just called. They tried to reach Dr. Adams, but he is still not back from lunch."

"I will handle this, Beth, thank you."

Suzy sat down behind her desk and called Adams on his private cell phone number. "I am not covering for him," she thought. "Let the Director handle it." Bitterness swept through her as she listened to the unanswered rings.

# 36

After Dr. Chen's sudden departure, Georgiana and Mark remained in the conference room, deciding their next move. George began to speak, and Mark motioned that they should step outside, not wanting to risk being overheard. As they left, George thanked the receptionist, mentioning they would return shortly. They asked her to have Dr. Adams call them as soon as he returned. Stacy jotted down George's cell phone number. Lieutenant Randall followed them outside and got into her car. They were getting used to their "shadow."

"Let's go over this place thoroughly," said George. "Call Wally and ask him to come here ASAP and request that he bring a forensics investigative team. I want computers, all videos of deliveries, the lab inventoried, everything."

George was convinced something wasn't quite right.

She said, "Dr. Chen was a little defensive. I want background checks on everyone, starting with Chen. I am going to check in with Fran and get an update. Maybe she knows something about the virus or whatever the hell we are dealing with."

Mark got on his cell phone and started things rolling with Wally. George was still talking to FBI Manhattan Field Office Director Fran Jacobs, when Mark got in the car and started the AC. It was steaming hot in the Mustang. George completed her call and then opened the door, took her jacket off, and laid it on the backseat.

Mark noticed that her blouse was damp, clinging to the curves of her breasts. Damn, she was beautiful. And smart. What a turn-on.

George said, "The meeting hasn't started yet. As soon as it does, Jacobs will call. Dr. Ambrose from the CDC will be conferencing in, as well, and we're going to coordinate operations. Director Bennett is there, as well as the police commissioner, a FEMA representative, the MTA, and perhaps some others. We'll know soon what's going on."

George continued, lifting her long hair off her neck, "Get this. Fran told me that the Century flight that made the emergency stop at BWI has another sick crew member. She was admitted to Miami University Medical Center. She has the same symptoms as the other flight attendant, Mrs. Ryan, who is being treated at Johns Hopkins."

Mark looked at George and said, "Not good. Maybe Homeland Security should hold that plane on the tarmac for a while?" Mark said, more as a statement than a question.

"Makes f-ing sense to me," she answered. The air conditioner was starting to work. George's cell phone rang. "Yes, Wally, what's up? Fast work. Thanks."

George turned to Mark and said, "Wally checked out Chen on a hunch. Did you know the NCS has been investigating Dr. Chen?"

Mark said quietly, "Bingo."

# 37

### The Mayor's Office

Georgiana and Mark were sitting in Mark's car, waiting for Jacobs to call. The AC was on high, keeping them cool. The meeting would be starting momentarily. George had briefed Jacobs earlier on their meeting with Dr. Chen and her NCS status, and Fran agreed that the lab should be scrutinized thoroughly. The facility housed many deadly viruses and toxic biological agents, therefore a logical starting point.

Dr. Ambrose came on the line, and introductions were made. It took only minutes for George and Mark to be conferenced in.

The Mayor began the meeting, asking each department head to report on any developments in their areas. Everyone acknowledged Mark and George, the FBI field agents presently in charge of the investigation, noting their current location at the Edgewood Laboratory.

Dr. Ambrose interrupted the meeting, excusing himself to take an urgent call.

Everyone heard him say, over the speakerphone, "Are you sure?" And after a pause, he said, "I know he is in isolation. Yes, we are checking on our inventory of anti-viral medications. How is your stock?" A few moments later, he responded, "Good. Thank you. I'll get back with you."

When he came back on the line, he said, "I just received information regarding the lab studies done on the patient most recently admitted to the Edgewood Medical Facility, Joey Caruso." The room became still.

"The maintenance worker from the subway, admitted to the Edgewood Medical Facility, has a virus, an exact replication of the one recently transported to the APG, a possible weaponized version of H5N1 virus, commonly known as bird flu. It was mutated by a team of virologists at," he hesitated, "a yet unnamed research facility, outside the US. This mutation allows the virus to pass from human to human, as opposed to its normal transfer from bird to human. The recent transport of this virus to the Edgewood Lab was for the purpose of further characterization and development of a treatment to prevent the transmission of the virus."

Everyone froze while listening to the scientific jargon, trying to digest its full meaning and implications.

"This virus is airborne transmitted, with flu-like symptoms occurring normally within three to four hours of exposure. Those suffering from the virus can develop varied symptoms. Breathing difficulties can develop with the onset of pneumonia. The immune system is threatened, and death can but does not always occur within a certain time frame, from twenty-four to forty-eight hours, or perhaps longer, depending on the condition of the host or patient."

Dr. Ambrose concluded, "Ladies and Gentlemen, in simple terms, we are dealing with a probable avian flu pandemic of uncertain proportion and scope."

# 38

Mike was sweating, tired of sitting in traffic. The air-conditioning was working, but not well enough. The sun was beating through the windows, and in standstill traffic, the heat was building.

The radio announcement was an alert about the heavy traffic.

"Due to the subway closure, all New York City residents are being asked to walk, take alternate transportation, or remain home until further notice. There is no reason for panic, and we ask that those planning on traveling into New York, do so only if absolutely necessary. There is no further information that we can report at this time. We will now continue with our regular programming."

"Crap," said Mike. It was getting closer to noon. He decided to head back home and call Johns Hopkins. He would try to get there tomorrow. Perhaps he could at least talk to Maggie or possibly see her. She was probably improving by now after getting hydrated. Maybe he was over reacting. There was nothing on the news about a bomb or any suspicious finding. Since 9/11 everyone panicked over the least little thing, himself included. He wanted to call, using his cell phone, but decided to wait until he got home. Making a turn in this traffic would require all of his attention. It would be a long crawl home, but he looked forward to getting there, being with the boys, especially if something was said at school that might scare them. He knew that would be what Maggie would want.

It took him a while to turn around, but he managed. It was just as busy going toward their apartment but at least he knew he would get there in a reasonable time frame. Pulling up in front of the building was a relief. Arnie was still there, standing under the awning, staring down the street.

"Nope, no news yet, Mr. Ryan. Guess it was impossible to drive out of town?"

"Yes, Arnie, it is a mess out there. I gave up but will try again tomorrow."

Mike hoped so anyway. He had lived in NYC a long time, but the uncertainties and the lack of information was beginning to raise many questions. As soon as Mike got into their apartment, he dialed Johns Hopkins, asking for the ER. Finally he was connected and asked for Jane Phillips.

"This is Jane Phillips," she answered. "May I help you?"

"Yes, this is Mike Ryan. You called me earlier this morning, about my wife Maggie. Can you please tell me how she is doing?"

"Mr. Ryan, your wife is in isolation. She is stable, and we have ordered lots of tests, and so far, the results have been inconclusive. But it appears that she has a virus of some type. Her lungs are congested, indicating pneumonia. She has a high fever, and we have placed her on antibiotics as well as an anti-viral medication. She is sleeping, and we are administering oxygen, to make her more comfortable." She was blunt but reassuring.

He said, "When can I bring her home?"

Ms. Phillips hesitated but said, "We can't be sure, Mr. Ryan. She is no doubt highly contagious, and we are monitoring her condition carefully."

"May I see her if I come there tomorrow? I tried to get out of the city today, but traffic was heavy."

Phillips said, "You can look at her through a window, for now. We are being cautious. I am sorry," she answered. "But if she improves, you may certainly visit her. I suggest you call before you make the drive." He was quiet.

Nurse Phillips said, "Mr. Ryan, she is getting the best of care. Please rest tonight, and let's hope she is better tomorrow so you can talk to her, at least on the phone."

Mike said, "You have my phone number if anything changes. Right?"

"Of course, Mr. Ryan."

"Thank you, I will call later this evening. Please tell her I love her and that I will see her tomorrow."

Mike hung up the phone, upset and confused, and just wanted one thing, to be with his wife. But he also understood she must be pretty sick, and somehow he felt a chill, feeling something was very wrong. He shook it off and knew he had to keep it together for the boys. He went to the family room, adjoining the kitchen, and turned on the TV set, hoping to hear any further news about the possibility of a citywide lockdown and the subway incident.

# 39

aptain Wesley kept the air-conditioning and ventilation systems running at full capacity while on the ground as they were waiting for the standby flight attendants to sub for Terry and Maggie. They couldn't fly without the FAA approved number of flight attendants for this equipment. Both standbys had checked in at operations and would arrive momentarily. Boarding would be slightly delayed, but hopefully they wouldn't be too late getting back to New York.

Flight Service was still cleaning the plane, loading fresh supplies, warm meals, and restocking the liquor drawers as the passengers on Flight 943, from MIA to LGA were waiting at the gate. Nearly all seats were booked.

John and Allen were in the cockpit, doing their pre-flight cross check, waiting for boarding to begin. They were concerned about Terry and Maggie, having received no further reports of their conditions. The hospitals were contacting the families, and John and Allen would be notified if there were updates.

John requested that maintenance check out the ventilation system and run it at maximum velocity to make sure it was thoroughly flushed with fresh air. No other passengers or crew, to his knowledge, had symptoms similar to Maggie's and Terry's, but he didn't want to take chances. They had checked with flight control for any news coming out of NYC, but so far, nothing conclusive, though the Mayor was to address the city momentarily. Traffic tie-ups and the usual announcements of "nothing to report" continued. However, there was speculation that there had been a possible terrorist attack on the subway but nothing definitive.

John and Allen called their wives upon arrival in Miami, reassuring them that things were fine and that they would be home as usual. Both were at home, watching the news, and didn't feel overly concerned. They were used to living in New York, where there were frequent alarmist news reports. Upon learning about the two flight attendants who had gotten sick, they did feel some concern. But they were "go with the flow" personalities, used to the life of military and commercial pilots, and there was always something to talk about when their husbands came home from a flight. John's wife, Dee Dee, had been a flight attendant back when they were called stewardesses, and nothing fazed her. She had carried many a barf bag in her flying days and handled more than her share of in-flight emergencies, from unruly passengers to dangerous turbulence and several emergency landings.

Captain Wesley still had that feeling of foreboding, an instinct he had learned when flying as a military pilot. Something wasn't right, and the fact that both Terry and Maggie were seriously ill was not a coincidence. But it would be business as usual as he pushed his negative thoughts aside. He was eager to get this "baby" back in the air, heading home.

He asked his copilot. "Okay, Allen, what do you think? The dispatcher says we are cleared to go. Your opinion?"

Allen, in his easygoing manner, said "Why not? Nothing to indicate that we stay. I'd like to get home tonight if possible."

John nodded. "Agreed." But he couldn't shake his uneasiness.

Allen turned to the doorway as the two FAs arrived, chatting about their first flight to NYC. They were fresh faced and bubbly, and the other crew members were waiting in the forward galley to greet them. After quick introductions, it was decided that the two novices would work in the rear cabin, with Justin and Jackie. Mary Ann, the more experienced of the crew, would man first class.

Captain Wesley and First Officer Allen met the two new girls as they passed the cockpit. Soon after, the gate attendant came out and got clearance to start boarding, and it was "standard operating procedure" at least for now.

Flight 943 nonstop to LaGuardia was scheduled for departure at 1:00 p.m. EDT. It was 12:30 p.m., and boarding would be starting momentarily.

Captain Wesley, without saying a word to Allen, picked up the mike and buzzed the gate agent, who answered right away.

"Yes, what is it, Captain? You ready for boarding?"

"No, don't let anyone on the plane. Scrub the flight. This plane is going into a service holding area. I won't put any of our passengers or crew at risk until we know fully what we are dealing with." Allen turned, looked at John, shaking his head, negative.

"What the fuck?" thought Allen.

"What should I tell the passengers?" asked the gate agent, irritated. .

"You can tell them that there is a mechanical problem and reschedule them on another flight, or tell them anything you want. But as captain, I have full responsibility for the safety of my crew and passengers, and it is my call. Got it?" He looked at Allen and could see he had Allen's support.

"I don't know if we have a problem, but if we do, I don't want to find out about it at thirty thousand feet."

"You got it, Captain," said the agent.

John's next move was to notify operations. They weren't going to like it, but tough shit. He told Allen to tell the crew what was going on. An overnight in Miami wouldn't be considered tough duty. John wanted to check on Terry and Maggie, anyway. He would check with the tower about where he could park the plane. It should go into an isolated holding "box" or other secure area of the airport.

Things could go from bad to worse fast, and he had to listen to his gut. It had gotten him through some dicey moments when flying C-130 transports in the air force. He wasn't going to ignore it now.

# 40

Suzy and Max spent that May Saturday morning making love in his king-sized bed at his spacious brick townhouse in Georgetown. She didn't stay at his place as often as he stayed at hers, but she felt comfortable in his home. She had left many of her personal belongings there, from a spare blow dryer and toothbrush, to sexy lingerie and gym clothes. He belonged to a gym, where they enjoyed working out together. Suzy did her light weight workout, and Max had a more strenuous workout, lifting heavy weights to maintain his trim military physique.

She had awakened Max that morning with feather light kisses to the back of his neck. They had slept spooned together, her naked body pressed against his strong warm back. They often woke in the night, made gentle love to each other, and then fell back to sleep. Their desperate need for each other had not diminished. Their passion grew, as they explored all ways of pleasuring each other. He loved her beautiful little ass, holding it against him, their intimate caresses and kisses, touching her intimately, and especially when she would pleasure him, sitting on top of him, controlling and moving him in and out of her at her whim, squeezing her muscles tight around him, making him beg her never to stop. She loved when he kissed her and moistened her secret place with his tongue. She was still wet from their lovemaking in the night.

As her morning kisses became more intense, she began to touch his body, between his legs, and Max reacted suddenly, rolling her over, holding her arms over her head, his mouth hard on hers. He opened her legs fiercely and shoved his huge hardness into her wet opening, and he wouldn't stop until she was coming. And he kept saying, "Tell me you love me, only me," and she said it over and over and over again, "I love you, Max—I love you, only you," until the waves of orgasm stopped, and then he came in her, the heat magnifying the waves of pleasure. They kissed and held each other, talking softly, loving each other, in real time, knowing it was forever.

Later, Suzy was in the shower, washing her hair, but she could hear his cell phone ring. Max was talking with someone, but she couldn't understand what was being said. He didn't get many calls on Saturdays, and she hoped he wasn't being called to work. Emergencies had come up before when he would have to report for duty. Fortunately it wasn't often. She cherished every moment they could spend together.

She stepped out of the shower, grabbed the soft gray towel that matched the dark gray-tiled bathroom, dried herself, and then wrapped the towel around her torso. Max had dressed and was in the kitchen, having promised to make her breakfast. She could smell the coffee and hear him busily preparing their eggs, toast and bacon.

Suzy picked up Max's cell phone from the night table. She brought up the call history and memorized the most recent phone number on the list. She grabbed her cell phone from her purse, which had caller ID blocked, and dialed the number. She didn't want Max to know how jealous she was, and she wanted to make sure it wasn't a woman who answered.

After several rings, a man answered, "Greg Hammond speaking."

Startled, Suzy said, "Oh, sorry, wrong number," and she ended the call. She would do some research to learn more about Greg Hammond. His name was unfamiliar to Suzy. She had met several of Max's friends at official functions, but she was pretty sure she had not met a Greg Hammond. Her curiosity had been piqued, and she wanted to know everything about Max. It could be anyone, but she had to be sure. Her paranoia was normal, considering Max's position, though she trusted him fully. She couldn't think of anything that might have made her suspicious of him, but who knows. He loved her. She believed in her heart that it was a true and real love. She knew that nothing was wrong, but it couldn't hurt to find out who this Greg person was.

Suzy slipped on a white fitted T-shirt, with no bra, and her gray yoga pants. She had put on a soft rose lip gloss, and her long black hair was still a little damp from her shower. As she walked into the kitchen, she found coffee waiting in a maroon mug on the granite countertop, with a maroon, blue, and gray plaid napkin placed next to it.

"Thank you, love," she said softly.

He turned away from the stove and noticed her sexy breasts, nipples erect through her thin T-shirt. He was getting hard again. Damn, he smiled inwardly.

"Who was on the phone?" she asked. "I heard it ringing when I was in the shower. I hope you don't have to work today."

"No," Max said, as he put the wheat bread slices in his stainless steel toaster oven. "It was just a reminder from my dentist about my checkup next week. No big deal."

"Oh, good," Suzy said, and walked over to see how the eggs were coming.

"Interesting," she thought.

# 41

Greg and Max found a private spot in the back of a small Greek restaurant tucked away on a side street near Greg's office. There were several comfortable booths to the right of the front door, a leather sofa and chairs with a coffee table in front of the window, and some small glass-topped tables in the back. It was a great place for coffee and delicious Greek specialties, including stuffed grape leaves, pita pies, and other traditional choices. Greg suggested they try the Kolatsio, a Greek snack, perfect for brunch or a main meal. Greg also chose the spinach pie and regular coffee, and Max decided on an egg and vegetable omelet with coffee, as well. The pretty waitress with a slight European accent took their order and said she would be back soon with coffee.

"Never tried this place," said Greg. "Thought it would be a nice change."

Max agreed. "Yes, it smells good in here. Hope she hurries with the coffee. And I am starved."

After the aromatic coffee was served in small china cups, Greg pulled out a sealed manila envelope and said, "Here is the report you wanted."

He handed it to Max, and Max opened it, pulled out the lengthy report, and started reading. Greg was silent, sipping his coffee. He was waiting for a reaction. Max calmly put the pages back in the envelope and asked Greg, "Did you verify this?" already knowing the answer.

"Yes, we have great analysts. It didn't take long for them to figure it out," he said. "Your girl is interesting. One of our agents in Hong Kong did a lot of research on her background." He hesitated. "We've added her to our watch list, Max."

"Fuck!" said Max, slamming the envelope down on the table, and several people sitting nearby turned and looked at him.

"Careful, buddy, hang tough here," Greg whispered. "You wanted to know, and we're glad you did, though I understand your shock."

"Hey, man, I love this girl, and I can't get my mind around this now." Max was both angry and worried. "She is in this thing, and it is obvious why. But she is in deep shit. They fucking knew how to bag her. God damn it, what the hell am I supposed to do now?"

"You say nothing, Max. Keep track of her—maybe you will learn something. We will do standard surveillance. She has an impeccable reputation, and hopefully we can keep her safe and try to understand what she's involved in, but it must be big. The numbers refer to a Swiss bank account with no name listed. A password is needed to access it. I can only speculate." He stopped with that thought.

"Our cipher people are always cautious when there is a specified date. There are adders or subtractors that could change the target date. Looks like we have several months. There must be someone or several 'someones' pulling the strings. With your help, we could get them."

"And nail Suzy too, right? Fuck you!" Max shouted. People were really starting to stare now, and Greg knew when to keep his mouth shut.

The food was served, and both ate silently. Max's appetite was gone.

"Let's get the hell out of here. I need a drink! " Max threw his napkin down and walked out.

Greg followed him, throwing some bills on the table as he left.

# 42

Wesley, Delaney, and the rest of the crew were at a hotel near the Miami International Airport. Operations was more than comfortable with John's decision to scratch the flight, especially since they had received a call ten minutes later from Homeland Security, grounding the flight. Wesley had made the right call. The rerouted passengers were disgruntled and complaining, but tough shit.

John and Allen, exhausted from the day's events, were eating dinner in Allen's room. Their eyes were glued to the television set.

The reporter was saying, "The number of those with flu-like symptoms is rising. Medical facilities are filling rapidly as the scope of the pandemic widens. Flights in and out of New York City have been cancelled, and the New York City subway system is shut down until further notice. New York City residents are being asked to remain at home unless it is an absolute emergency." John and Allen just looked at each other.

"Let's call the hospital again about Terry."

"Yes," nodded John, and he added, "Let's check on Maggie as well."

"Maybe I can talk with Terry's parents," Allen said.

"I need to call my wife, too. Who knows how long we are going to be stuck here?" John stated. "Operations said to sit tight, so that is what we are going to do."

He knew the airline backed up his decision to abort the flight. His concerns mounted when he learned that Homeland Security also made the call to ground the flight.

John grabbed his cell phone and called his wife, Dee Dee. "Hey, sweetheart, are you okay?"

"Yes, John, how are you doing? I have been so worried. The news is scary." She sounded a little shaky, not usual for her.

John reassured her, "I'm okay, baby. We are just going to be stuck here for a while as a precaution." She wanted to know if he had eaten. She had prepared dinner for them, but she would save the leftovers for tomorrow.

"Have you talked to the kids?" he asked.

"Yes, Abby is fine. She called, concerned about us. I reassured her, but I'm glad she and Cindy don't live in the city. I left a voice mail for Cindy. She'll call back soon."

He said, "Good. Just remind them to stock up on necessities, enough for two weeks. They're smart and will be okay, but it is good to touch base with them." He asked, "How are the grocery supplies?"

"Fine, John. I did a large shopping on Saturday. We have enough groceries for at least a week or more," she answered, puzzled by that question.

He said, "Maybe buy some extras, if you can, just to have on hand, like canned goods, extra flour and basics."

Dee Dee said, "I shopped again this morning. I had forgotten a few things. Some of the store shelves seemed a little bare."

John said, "I'm glad you bought some extras. Stores may run out of necessities if people start to panic.""

But she said, jokingly, "We have a good supply of scotch."

He laughed and then said, "Cool, baby."

"When will you be home?" Dee Dee knew the answer already.

"I am not sure, but I will stay in close touch, sweetheart. Don't go out unless you have to, understood? And on second thought, call the girls again. Tell them to do the same. Have them stock up then sit tight until we see where this is going. "

"Yes, I'll call them right away. Cindy may be home by now," said Dee Dee, feeling even more frightened.

"Do you have any news about Maggie or Terry?" she asked.

"Allen is checking on them now, but so far no updates," he answered. "I better go, but call me if you need anything. Try not to worry, and remember, I love you, baby."

Dee Dee said, "I love you too, John. Be safe. I miss you so much."

"I miss you, too, baby. I wish I was with you right now. You know my favorite color, right?" he asked.

She said, "Black satin?"

He laughed, saying, "Yes, or nothing at all." He smiled when he heard her giggle, but he hated being away, especially during this unprecedented crisis. He had heard of pandemics, but he wasn't quite sure what it all meant. And was this an attack or just a severe virus?

After hanging up, he listened to Allen, who was talking to Terry's father. His face looked grim.

"Fuck," thought John.

Wherever this was going, it was not going to be good. He was starting to wonder not when he would get home, but if he would get home.

John looked at the text he was receiving. It was from Century Air operations.

"DHS confirms shutdown of all NYC airports, plus New Jersey, Philadelphia, Baltimore, Chicago, and Miami. More information as available."

"Shit! Damn!"

He turned to tell Allen, just as breaking news was announced on the television. He hoped this was some kind of bureaucratic over reaction, but his gut was telling him that a shit storm was coming, big time.

# 43

Suzy was sound asleep when she was startled awake by the distinctive ring of her encrypted phone. She knew it was the Organization.

"Yes, what is it?"

The familiar voice replied, "You are under scrutiny. Some as yet unknown operatives are looking into your background, specifically foreign ties and activities. You are involved with someone, a certain US Army Lieutenant Colonel. Is that correct?

Suddenly wide-awake, Suzy responded, "Yes, why?" Her stomach lurched.

The male voice, indistinguishable accent, continued, "You are to cut ties with him. Is that clear?"

It was not a question; it was an order. She didn't tell him about the Greg Hammond incident. It seemed like a moot point now, but she was scared, and she couldn't believe Max was somehow a danger to her mission or to her. How could he be? He loved her. At least he said he did. Had she somehow unknowingly revealed information? Or was it a setup? Was she his "assignment"? Her gut was wrenching as her thoughts raced. She considered all possibilities, even the most unimaginable ones.

"If I do so abruptly, it might raise suspicions," Suzy pointed out.

The response was as expected. "Nothing must impede our mission, and if you wish for a positive outcome, shall we say, you will follow instructions immediately."

"My fear is that it will alert him. Please allow me a few weeks to disengage. I will figure out a way. Much is at stake for me, as well."

"Eliminate the Lieutenant Colonel from your life, or we will," he stated.

Chills ran through Suzy's body and she began to shake uncontrollably.

Silence followed on the other end. Then the sinister voice said, "Let's accelerate our plan. 4 .6. Got it?" It was a threat. "Then if he somehow obtained information, we have changed the game."

"Yes, 4.6. Got it."

The line went dead.

# 44

Suzy got to Max's townhouse an hour before he would get home from his Ft. Meade office. She had shopped for groceries and was going to prepare dinner for him to celebrate their five-month anniversary. She had his key and security code and let herself in, her arms tired from carrying the wine and several parcels. He had seemed distant lately, distracted about something. She had brushed it off as his preoccupation with his work. Maybe she was his "work." Good job, Max, she thought. I fell for it, big time. Her anger was building. She heard the garage door open and knew she had to put her worries aside. It was easy to do because Max was the only happiness she had ever known, and in the deepest part of her being, she knew she could trust him with her life.

Max came in the door off the garage and heard Suzy in the kitchen. He had been looking forward to the evening, thinking of her delicious naked body all day. She was slicing vegetables when he came up behind her, wrapped his left arm around her, pulled her against him, while at the same time sweeping aside her long hair, and placing gentle, wet kisses on her slender neck.

She sighed, leaning against him, her back to his chest, saying, "Max, you're going to make me cut myself."

He reached around with one hand, grabbed her breast, and said, "Put the knife down."

She turned, facing him, their lips meeting. Their deep kisses and touches were uncontrolled as they pushed against each other. She could feel his arousal through his slacks, and she touched him, making him even harder. He backed away, reluctantly, and said, "Baby, let me shower and I'll be right back."

Suzy was breathless from his kisses and his touch. She smiled at him and said, "Yes, go ahead. I'll get dinner started, then we can share some wine."

Suzy put the vegetables and marinated chicken in a casserole dish and placed it in the oven. She made a tossed garden salad and set the table with fresh flowers and candles. She found the chilled bottle of Riesling in the refrigerator, opened it, and poured the pale yellow liquid into a tall wine glass. The shower was still running as she walked into the steamy bathroom. She could see his image through the glass door, leaning against the wall, letting the hot water flow down his back. He turned around and shut the water off. Opening the shower door, he grabbed a thick towel from the towel rack and began drying himself. Suzy couldn't stop admiring his muscular body and noticed he was still turned on.

"Darling, have a sip," as she offered the glass to him.

He wrapped the towel around his waist, then took a generous sip of the refreshing wine, and set the wine glass on the countertop. She had on his favorite outfit. He loved her in casual low-cut jeans and sweater, and her wedged sandals. He tossed the towel onto tile floor and grabbed Suzy, kissing her hard, pulled her sweater up, and licked the delicious mounds of her breasts, pushing them together, pulling her bra down to suck each of her erect nipples. God, she wanted him. She was holding his head against her as he was licking and sucking each breast, her breathing rapid.

She stopped him, grabbed his face, and kissed him, her tongue in his mouth, and then grabbing his cock, bent down, her back to the mirror, Suzy took his hardness in her mouth, and Max gasped, saying "Oh my God, baby." And he watched her in the mirror, which intensified his excitement. She didn't want to stop licking, kissing, and tasting him, holding his body tight in her hands. He belonged only to her. But he forcefully grabbed her, unzipped her jeans, turned her around, slid her jeans and thong panties down, and bent her over the counter and found her wetness with his finger. Then he entered her completely. Suzy was breathing so hard, and he couldn't stop, moving in and out of her with unimaginable raw pleasure, lifting her sweater, tearing her bra off, playing with her breasts. They both came violently, his body shuddering. His breathing was still heavy. Slowly, he began light kisses to her delicate shoulders and neck, and turned her around. Suzy bent down to lick him, tasting their intermingled love, and he pulled her up, kissed her mouth, wanting only Suzy forever, and his heart was aching.

He didn't know any reality but the now, and he didn't know that her heart was aching, as well, wondering what was the reality.

# 45

Suzy and Max had spent a wonderful Memorial weekend together, swimming on Saturday and relaxing by the pool. On Sunday, they had gone to Annapolis, walked around the shops at the harbor, and enjoyed a romantic dinner at one of their favorite restaurants. They sat on the patio, overlooking the water, eating off each other's plates, drinking wine, just enjoying being together.

It was a special weekend, and Suzy had loved every moment but knew she had to be guarded. She had looked into who "Greg Hammond" was. She was relieved to find out that he had graduated from West Point the same year that Max had graduated. But why wouldn't Max have told her? Why did he say it was a dental appointment reminder? Suzy couldn't find any further information on Greg Hammond, which was perplexing. Max was especially attentive and loving. She had been watching him, looking for changes in his behavior toward her, but she found none. Though she knew something was wrong. The instructions to end the relationship were based on facts unknown to her, and it was imperative that she follow their orders. Maybe they were just being cautious, considering Max's position. She had tried to be her natural self with him, which was easy because she loved him deeply and fully, and in her heart, Suzy believed that he felt the same about her. She knew this was to be their last weekend together. How could she give him up? She knew the answer.

As they drove back to Suzy's condo, both were looking forward to their night together. Their sexual tension had been building throughout the day, even though they had made passionate love that morning. Max couldn't erase the image of Suzy, earlier in the day, in her very brief aqua bikini, low-cut with ties on each side of the bottom, and the sexy top that nearly exposed her exquisite breasts and delicious erect nipples, pushing them nearly out of the suit. Her skin had tanned, and he loved the contrast of the tan against the delicate white skin covered by her bikini. They had swum together, hugging and playing in the water, diving deeply, watching each other as the sun glistened on their shapes. He was an athlete, moving gracefully, and she loved watching him, his strong shoulders, his broad defined chest, narrow hips, and muscular legs. His strength and masculinity were huge turn-ons. They had flirted and stolen kisses, trying not to be blatant around the others at the community pool, but it was well known that they were an "item" and the attraction they felt was obvious.

That evening, as they walked into her kitchen, they stopped to share a deep kiss. Max grabbed Suzy's hand and began leading her up the curved hardwood staircase. He led her to her bedroom and began undressing her.

She was wearing only her lacy black panties and bra when she said, "Max, I would like to shower, okay?"

He said, "Yes, baby," and she embraced him, giving him a lingering kiss, his arms enveloping her.

She giggled as she pulled away and said, "I'll be back soon."

"Hurry, baby, I can't wait much longer."

Suzy went into the bathroom. She threw her sexy panties and bra on the cream-colored marble vanity and turned on the shower. It took a moment for the water to warm, and Suzy stepped in. Grabbing the body gel, she began washing, and then suddenly Max was behind her, naked, his hands washing her, his arms around her, and she turned to face him, their kisses longing. Water was cascading down their bodies as they embraced.

She lathered her hands and began washing Max, making him turn and face the spray of water, and she slowly washed his shoulders, his back, and his hips, her hands touching him in every private place, feeling complete ownership of every part of him. She began washing and stroking his enormous hard cock, and all of his masculinity, and then she bent down and kissed him, her hands at play with all of him. He pulled her up and kissed her, his tongue in her mouth, his hand between her legs, touching her, saying love words, wanting her. With the water streaming over them, he lifted her, her legs wrapping around him.

He slid into her, and she moved up and down against him, moaning in his ear, "Oh Max, my love, I need you. Don't ever stop," as she had orgasm after orgasm.

He could feel her body responding to his hardness, tightening around his cock, and it drove him wild. He was thrusting and thrusting into her, and he came, exciting her even more. They had no awareness of anything, only each other, nothing separating one from the other. They were kissing, letting the cool water run over them.

Later, they lay in bed, naked, knowing they would make love again. They slept, wrapped together, and when they awoke, around midnight, they were ravenous. Suzy brought a tray of wine, cheese, and assorted crackers to bed, and they ate and sipped wine while watching television, enjoying being together, smiling, touching, kissing, sharing bites, and just being close. Afterward, they snuggled against each other, sharing their breaths, both happier than either had ever known.

Suzy was nestled against Max, his arm around her, her leg thrown over his. As Max fell asleep, he whispered,

"Talk to me, Suzy."

She answered, "I love you, Max."

Suzy knew this moment in time would be etched in her memory and heart forever. Max was her only everlasting love. He owned her, body and soul.

# 46

### The Mayor's Office

Tom Bennett, the Regional Homeland Security Director, began discussing the All Saints Hospital patients. The lab results indicated an unknown virus, but no clinical certainty of its type. Four other patients had been admitted there also, making the count seven, so far. He and Dr. Ambrose were deciding whether to transfer the patients from All Saints to the Edgewood Medical Facility. He had spoken to the hospital administrator, Jim Lucas, who wanted them moved to another facility to insure safety of their current patients and staff. Dr. David Grant, the All Saints ER director, had been adamant about protecting the hospital from the potential rapid spread of this dangerous virus.

Bennett was firm. "The patients must not be transported anywhere. We are not moving anyone at this point. We must keep risk of further exposure to a minimum. We will mobilize FEMA, notify the Health and Human Services Director, the National Guard, and all state governors. All cities with public transportation systems should be placed on high alert status, and a thorough search should be made for any suspicious packages or containers." He continued, "Dr. Ambrose, I assume the CDC will notify all medical facilities."

Dr. Ambrose said, "Yes, systems are in place for such notification. We will start working immediately on a vaccine. Several pharmaceutical companies will begin the manufacture of a vaccine as well."

They all recognized the inability to secure the United States against the use of a bio-weapon or toxic agent. There had been great concerns about an attack of this nature, but this attack was more terrifying than any had expected.

Ambrose continued, "We need to alert the public so they can prepare. We must close schools, cancel events, and warn of possible disruption of services. The general public must be informed that they will need to buy extra supplies and items necessary for basic survival. We cannot predict the duration of this pandemic. We must be candid in all communications."

The Mayor said, "Yes, we'll include safety information in my news conference as a precaution. I want to discourage panic. We'll remind them to check the NYC website which has guidelines for dealing with pandemics. Mary and I will discuss, along with you, Tom, whether to shut down the financial district to minimize traffic in and out of the city."

Bennett asked, "Agent Reed, has Quantico come up with anything on the canister?"

She answered by phone, "It tests positive for H5N1. We have nothing of consequence on the canister itself, but it appears to have been manufactured in the US. It resembles a common aerosol spray can used in fumigation applications, available in many hardware and pet stores, or even veterinarian offices."

"Keep me informed," he requested.

"Yes, sir," she responded.

Mayor Donnelly asked Bennett, "Will you notify the Secretary of the Department of Homeland Security and the President?"

"Yes," he said, "that was my next move, Mr. Mayor." And turning from him, he pulled out his secure cell phone.

"Jesus," said Donnelly, under his breath. "We have a fucking bird flu outbreak in fucking New York City."

George and Mark were listening raptly to the discussions, realizing a terrorist attack had occurred. The terrorist was perhaps homegrown, with easy access to the virus at the APG. Terrorist operations can be extremely elusive, especially if there are a small number of clandestine perpetrators involved. The magnitude of the attack was not anything that they expected. The full nature and implications of the expanding crisis were difficult to grasp.

Mayor Donnelly would release a statement to assure the populace that steps were being taken to contain the pandemic as quickly as possible. Those with symptoms were to seek immediate medical treatment. Those working in the city were to leave work, if possible, in an orderly fashion until further notice. All medical facilities and hospitals would be notified by the CDC.

Mayor Donnelly faced a great dilemma. Shutting down the city seemed out of the question. To do so could be catastrophic, and also, he would be giving the terrorist or terrorist group exactly what they wanted. He remembered 9/11 and the courage of the New York City residents. He knew they would handle this emergency bravely as well. But this was different, at least for now. He must lock down New York City, including Amtrak and all airports. The spread of this contagion must be halted.

Director Jacobs spoke up. "Georgiana, do you have anything to add in regards to the investigation?"

George said, "Yes, Ms. Jacobs. We have pertinent information that you need to know, before ending this meeting, if I may."

She filled them in on the FBI findings and the ensuing investigation, starting at Edgewood. Everyone knew what had to be done. The heads of departments would remain in the Mayor's office and use it as a "war room."

The Mayor knew the virus had begun to spread throughout the city, state, or God knows where else. He called his press secretary, asking him to arrange for emergency television and radio announcements. The information would be available on the New York City website as well. FEMA and the Secretary of the Department of Homeland Security would handle the national news reports. His assistant, Nancy, came in, and they began working on the most difficult speech he would ever deliver.

They were under attack by an invisible enemy, and panic must be averted. He would be relentless in hunting down whoever was responsible for this reprehensible act of terrorism. He gathered his strength and would rely on God's direction for this one. He began composing the rough draft.

# 47

Without realizing it, Dr. Grant had fallen asleep at his desk, and the knock on his office door startled him. It was Chris.

He rubbed his eyes, ran his hands through his hair, and said, "What time is it?"

Before she could answer, the phone rang. It was Jim Lucas, the hospital administrator.

"Dave, we have some news from Dr. Ambrose, at the CDC."

"Go ahead," Dave said.

"We are dealing with an avian flu outbreak, a mutant strain." Jim paused.

"Damn! Any word on moving these people to Edgewood?"

"No can do. They want to keep us isolated and not risk further exposure, if possible."

Grant was pissed. "What else?"

"We will have more patients as this spreads. It appears to be weaponized, mutated to spread rapidly with a short incubation time frame."

"What about anti-viral meds?" asked Dave.

"The CDC is gathering supplies. They will be distributed, starting with New York City hospitals, considered the 'Impact Zone' or 'Strike Point' then to other sites as this pandemic escalates."

"I guess we have no choice," said Dave.

"Correct," said Jim.

Dave was quiet. "Are we getting routine food and medical supply deliveries?"

"Yes," said Jim. "No problems, so far."

"Our staff is bone tired."

Jim said, "We are working on it. We are currently in lockdown. Only staff and severely ill patients are allowed to enter our facility. Security is at all entrances, including the employee entrance."

"Have you told Frank?"

"Yes, he knows."

"I'll call him. I need to check patient status," Dave stated.

Jim said, "It's not good."

Jim continued, "I've called a meeting of department heads for 4:00 p.m. My office. We need a plan to provide care and deal with this crisis, short and long term. I need everyone's input on this."

Dave said, "I'll see you at four."

Dave was thinking of the effects of this far-reaching pandemic on food, medical supplies, and other essentials. How far would it spread, and how long would it last? He had no answers, only questions. Grocery stores and drug stores would be packed. Hospitals would be overrun with sick patients. He wondered how long basic supplies would last, and he envisioned the potential desperation and the eventual chaos that would result. New York was the epicenter, and the storm was spreading.

"God help us," said Dave as he hung up the phone. Chris was sitting on the sofa, transfixed by what Dave had said. He sat next to her, pulling her close. Their lips met, as he held her, no words needed.

Dave said to Chris, "I need to check on our staff, get updates on patient status, and may I ask you to make sure the staff lounges are comfortable and ready for breaks? We're stretched thin."

"Yes, Dave." He could tell she was scared. He also knew she was on game and he could count on her.

"How are you feeling, sweetheart?" he asked. He could see dark circles under her eyes.

"I'm all right, just a little tired. That's all. I am worried about you," she said.

"No worries, Chris. We will get through this thing, but we both know what 'pandemic' means."

"Yes," she said.

He kissed her again, held her tightly against him, and then said, "Keeping our heads will keep others on track." He knew she would have no problem with that.

"Come on, baby," he said, opening the office door.

# 48

M ike was transfixed by Mayor Donnelly's news conference. The Mayor was at the podium, in front of City Hall, surrounded by representatives of various agencies, including the Department of Homeland Security, the NYC Police Commissioner, the FBI Regional Director, the Department of Defense, FEMA and other high ranking officials. The words weren't quite making sense. Mike had some knowledge regarding viruses and specific strains, and of recent reports of avian flu and its transmission studies. The more he listened, the more his concerns mounted. The Mayor said that cases of avian flu had been reported by several hospitals in the New York City area. Other cities in New Jersey and Florida were reporting similar outbreaks. New York had declared a state of emergency, and flights in and out of New York City were cancelled.

The Mayor was asking the general public to remain calm but to use caution and stay at home, if possible, to prevent further spread of the contagion. No one was to leave home unless absolutely necessary. All government officials were to continue to report to work. Further reports and instructions would be forthcoming as more information became available. Stations would be set up by FEMA where protective face masks would be distributed. This was simply a precaution. The National Guard was being mobilized if needed. Mike wondered what that meant.

"There is nothing definite to report about this being a possible terrorist action. The FBI is investigating and will provide updates as soon as possible."

The Mayor wanted to quell fears as much as possible.

After the Mayor again stressed that everyone remain calm, the director of FEMA took the podium. He explained further about face mask distribution and gave a government website that provided detailed instructions on dealing with pandemics. He also asked neighbors to help neighbors and for families to share supplies.

Mike was stunned. He grabbed the phone and called Pembrooke Academy. He spoke with the receptionist, asking about the children, and whether they would be dismissed early. She said no, but the school was aware of the subway incident, and they were monitoring all news reports. The administration was evaluating options that would best safeguard the children and she assured him that he would be notified if there were any changes in school policy.

He slammed the phone down and called Johns Hopkins, asking for the Isolation Unit.

"ICU isolation desk, may I help you?"

"Yes, I'm Mike Ryan, Maggie, uh, Margaret Ryan's husband. How is she?" The clerk put him on hold as she connected him to the charge nurse.

"Barbara Knox speaking."

Mike repeated his query, "How is Maggie Ryan, my wife? This is Mike Ryan."

"Mr. Ryan, she is holding her own, though she has a fever and pneumonia. However, she is not worsening, which is encouraging."

"May I see her?" He was plaintive, though he knew the answer.

"No, your safety must be ensured. Maggie is getting excellent care. And you realize Maggie would want you to stay put. Correct?"

Mike didn't answer. She was correct. "Please tell her I called. May I call again?"

"Of course, Mr. Ryan."

"Ms. Knox, do you have other patients arriving with Maggie's symptoms?"

"None at present, Mike. And call me Barbara."

"What has the lab determined regarding Maggie's illness?"

"We are repeating the lab studies, but we have essentially confirmed the avian flu diagnosis. But you know Maggie is strong, young, and has no current health problems. Correct?"

"Yes, very healthy," he responded, more hopeful.

"Then we have optimism about her prognosis. You did know that Maggie is pregnant."

Mike sat back in his chair in stunned silence.

# 49

Donna had taken the baby to her mother's home after Marty called about Joey being sick. It had been a happy day until then. Before the call, Donna had straightened the house, cleaned up the kitchen, and showered before Rosa woke up. Then she was busy, feeding the baby some rice cereal and baby food. Rosa had made sweet cooing noises and sighs, and smiled at her, which made Donna melt.

But now she was scared. She gathered some of the baby's things and drove straight to her mom's. Thank goodness her mom was home. They had been watching the news, which made Donna worry even more. She kept replaying, in her mind, the words that Joey had spoken when he had called. He sounded a little worried, but okay, strong, her Joey. After Marty called, her doubts had grown. Where did they take Joey? Why didn't Marty tell her? It was just a precaution, he had said. She fully understood that she needed to keep the baby safe. She hated hospitals anyway, always fearful of germs and catching something, but she would give anything to be with him. Donna had dialed Joey's cell phone number, but she only got his voice mail. He probably was busy, getting tests or being checked.

Donna and her mom, Elaine, had played with Rosa, then fed her again, and put her down in the port-a-crib that her mom kept in the spare room. Elaine loved the baby and doted on her. Life had been empty since Ed had died. It was sudden. He had a massive heart attack, and abruptly, life changed. The baby had filled some of the void though her mom's heart was broken forever. Donna loved seeing her mom holding Rosa and the joy that it brought to her.

Donna and her mom kept the TV on, listening for further developments. It was more confusing now, and the subway was still shut down. The buses were running, which prevented traffic from coming to a total standstill. They both wanted things to be back to normal.

Donna said, "Mom, maybe I should call Marty. I need to know about Joey."

Elaine said, "It can't hurt to call. Do you know which hospital Joey went to?"

"No, I can't remember exactly. I think Marty just said they were taking him to the doctor, just to get checked. And why hasn't Joey called?" Donna wondered, aloud. "I'm calling Marty," Donna decided and grabbed her cell phone from her jeans pocket. She found Marty's office number in her contact list. She was glad Joey had given that to her. He was always thoughtful about things like that. She heard the ringing.

A man's voice said, "Officer Lewis speaking."

"This is Donna Caruso. I am trying to reach Marty, please." Her voice sounded nervous.

"Are you Joey's wife, ma'am?"

"Yes, sir," she answered awkwardly.

"Ma'am, Marty had to step away from his desk. May I help you?" He was being very formal.

"Well, I want to know how Joey is doing. Marty said he went to the doctor. Is he okay? I can't reach Joey on his cell phone, and I am getting worried." Donna couldn't hold back her tears.

"Mrs. Caruso, please be calm. Everything is under control. Your husband got nauseated, and Marty decided Joey needed to be checked out, as a precaution, and we haven't heard back yet. But I know he is getting good care. As soon as I hear anything, I'll call you right away, okay? There is no reason to be overly concerned, but I understand." His voice was comforting. Donna felt better. "Where are you?" he asked.

"I'm at my mom's, with Rosa, our baby," Donna said. She gave him her cell phone number and her mother's number.

"Good, you just sit tight there. Okay?"

"Yes, sir. Just tell Marty I called, please, and to call me when he can," she requested.

"Will do, Mrs. Caruso." Officer Lewis hung up.

He thought he had handled that the best way he could. What he had not told her was that Marty and several of the other maintenance guys had gotten sick, as well, plus his partner, Jack. There were only a few left in the subway station office, including several passengers who happened to be on the platform at the time of the quarantine. They were all waiting for answers. Right now, no one knew what was going on or why. All Lewis knew was that he was scared shitless. Who would be next?

# 50

D r. Ambrose was getting regular updates about the virus and the measures being taken to halt its spread. He was deep in thought, analyzing all available information. Numerous medical facilities in New York and several in New Jersey were beginning to report patients' arrivals, all with similar symptoms as those who had been in direct contact with the deadly viral release in the New York City subway station.

An advisory was received from Chicago regarding a dozen possible cases of the "flu" in question. Tests were being conducted to confirm if they were in fact the avian flu.

Miami University Medical Center had informed the CDC that they had received, in addition to the flight attendant, several other patients with the same symptoms, all of whom had been on Flight 227. They were quarantined.

The reports continued to trickle in, and now that the avian virus had been identified, time required for diagnosis confirmation was shortened. Dr. Ambrose's concerns were growing as each report came in, showing the steady rise in the number of cases and a broadened geographic spread of the pandemic. He had studied the avian flu virus, and from all indications, it is rare and only transmitted from wild birds to domesticated birds, like turkey, chicken, and ducks, and then to humans, if eaten. Then pandemic risk can follow. When bird flu affects humans, it is often deadly. The mutated weaponized version of avian flu could continue mutating. The kill potential was vast and out of his range of expertise.

With advanced technology and a fast news cycle, he was hopeful that there might be the greater likelihood of containment of this apparent mutating virus. Keeping people at home, informed, for an as yet undetermined time frame, might save some lives, but many would still die or become severely ill, especially the very young, the elderly, or others at high risk. Outbreaks were unpredictable.

The CDC and the World Health Organization had experience tracking pandemics, going back to the 1918 worldwide flu outbreak, which was severe and deadly. Ambrose was well read on the Spanish flu, as it was called. Its duration had been approximately two years, and it killed between fifty and one hundred million people worldwide. Three percent of the entire world population had died, though 27 percent had been infected.

Dr. Ambrose also knew that some pandemics were more severe than others. This one, he was certain, would be one of the more severe. By definition, influenza pandemics occurred when a new variant of the influenza virus was transmitted to humans from another animal species, like the most recent 2009 flu pandemic. That one seemed to affect only young people.

All Dr. Ambrose could do was keep the Health Alert Network, Homeland Security, and FEMA alerted to the extent of this ongoing crisis and pray that it could be contained. The CDC was tracking the evolving pandemic and would start the process of developing a vaccine. Time was critical. It would take a minimum of three months to produce the needed vaccine. By then, he feared it might be too late.

# 51

Max felt close to Suzy throughout the entire weekend, though he had been observing her, trying to note any deviation from her normal behavior. At times she seemed distracted, but this wasn't necessarily unusual. Her work could be intrusive, and she often had to answer e-mails and take a few hours on a Saturday to finish up required reports or do some reading. Sometimes she mentioned non-classified work issues she was dealing with, but not often.

Only once had Suzy had complained to Max about the lab director, Dr. Adams. He was a demanding, egotistical personality type. Even though she was assistant director of Edgewood Labs, there had been difficulties. Max quizzed her playfully, but was inwardly jealous. Apparently the man was a skirt chaser, and Suzy had been his target at one time. She eventually caught on, but Max could tell it bothered Suzy, deep down, that Adams had deceived her. Although implied, she didn't really say she had cared for him, but Max knew something significant had happened between them. She had alluded to the fact that they had been in a relationship, or at least, Suzy had felt they were in a relationship, but she was let down when she realized that she was just another of his conquests. She never admitted any of this to Max, but he sensed what went down. He wanted to punch the guy out and would have to resist doing so if they ever crossed paths.

It had been difficult for Max not to broach the topic that weighed heavily on him. He wanted to say, "Baby, tell me everything and let me help you," but he couldn't. Not yet. He wanted no harm to come to her or her family, and he felt he had a little more time. He knew the risks were high, but he wanted to assist in the capture of those who were behind the threats. He had to trust Greg and not let Suzy become aware of what he had been told. He didn't know what they wanted her to do, but he was concerned.

They shared a lingering good-bye kiss that Monday evening, and Suzy embraced him so very tightly, not wanting him to leave. He responded, holding her close to him, as close as possible, feeling her love and passion all mixed together.

"I'll call you when I get home," he said, and pulled away, though he did not want to leave.

She was quiet, just smiled at him, and said, "You know I love you, right?"

Max said, "Yes, I know." He looked deeply in her eyes, got into his Mercedes, and backed down the driveway.

Suzy stood in the driveway and watched his car slowly pulling away. She waved to him, as she always did when he left. This time she wondered when she would see him again. She went into the house with tears streaming down her face. They would not stop. She went upstairs, fell across her bed, and cried until she fell asleep.

The ringing phone on the night table woke her. She looked at caller ID, knew it was Max, and said a breathless, "Hey."

Max said, "Will you marry me, Suzy?"

"Yes," she answered, with no hesitation. She could feel her heart beating.

"That's all I need to know."

# 52

Suzy had not answered her phone or e-mails all day, missing several calls from Max. She had not had time to call him back. The trip to her mother's had taken longer than expected, plus the drive back had seemed to take forever. Then, after sending the e-mail from Eric's laptop, the fucking FBI showed up. She shouldn't have been surprised, but she had not wanted to deal with them. Damn! How did they get to Edgewood so fast? She hoped she had handled the questioning without raising suspicions. She felt unnerved by the morning's events. Her thoughts were spinning, but she had to maintain her composure, somehow.

She needed to talk with Dr. Adams as soon as possible. She checked with Beth regarding his whereabouts. She hoped he had returned by now.

Beth said, "Yes, he is in his office."

"Thanks," she said, and walked down the hall, knocked on his door, and entered without waiting for an answer.

He looked up as she walked in. "Dr. Adams, I hope things went well with your son," she said sarcastically.

"You bitch," he thought.

"Yes, things went perfectly. Catch me up on what has been going on around here," he asked.

"I've been trying to reach you. You obviously turned off your cell phone. Didn't Beth give you my message?" she asked, very pissed off.

"Yes, but I have been busy," he answered, indifferently. "What is of such critical importance that you interrupt me while I was taking care of family business?"

Suzy noticed his rumpled hair and somewhat dazed look. She hoped he had enjoyed his little tryst with his slut of the day, while she was here doing his job of dealing with the FBI. What a prick.

Dr. Adams could see the look of disdain in Suzy's eyes. He should never have gotten involved with her, but damn, she was a great lay, and so gorgeous. Too bad she thought he was serious. He gave her the assistant director's position—what more could she want? Isn't that why she screwed him in the first place? She was smart and good at her work. Too good. But better get back to the business at hand.

"Again, what has been going on? Any results on the lab samples or anything from Quantico on the canister?" he asked.

"First of all, two agents from the FBI were here, looking for you and asking me all kinds of questions. I referred them back to you," she stated. "They are checking out any possible leads on the materials found in the New York City subway this morning."

He asked, "The FBI visit sounds like SOP. Do we have results back?"

"Yes, it's H5N1, and according to the lab at Quantico, the canister, so far, can't be traced, but Homeland Security has been notified," she stated.

"Damn, just damn." Then he asked, "How is the subway maintenance guy they brought down from New York? Did he test positive for the H5N1?" The daze was gone now. He buzzed Beth. "Bring me some coffee. Now!"

Suzy continued, "The worker, Mr. Caruso, has tested positive. He is very sick but stable for the moment. He had direct contact with the canister, first exposure. The virus has also spread to others, including those exposed while in the subway and others with whom they had contact. The CDC chemists and our lab staff worked together and came up with the identification fairly quickly."

Dr. Adams said, "We have samples of H5N1 in storage, as I recall. Have we started working on those yet?" He obviously had not ordered any work to be done.

She answered curtly, "No, but we should begin developing a vaccine, ASAP, agreed? Let's stress that this will be a joint effort of our people and those from the CDC. This particular virus spreads rapidly, and the faster we begin developing the vaccine, the better."

"Yes, of course. That was my next concern." He nodded agreement. Adams said, "Arrange an immediate staff meeting. I'll prepare the agenda. Let me know when everyone is ready."

"Fine," answered Suzy. Beth came in with the coffee as Suzy was leaving his office.

Suzy went directly to the lab and called the staff into the large meeting room, adjacent to the laboratory. About twenty were present. She said Dr. Adams had some announcements and would be in shortly. She stepped into the hallway and called him on the intercom, saying that they were waiting.

Adams breezed in, his I-Pad in hand. He stood at the front of the room, cleared his throat, and began by congratulating them on defining the variant H5N1 influenza virus and then instructed them to begin working on a vaccine. This would take a great deal of time and effort but that was to be their priority. Developing a vaccine was critical. They were to work jointly with the CDC and the FBI, and he stressed full cooperation to facilitate a quick result.

Many had questions, which Adams couldn't answer. All had seen the news reports of the outbreak and that it was possibly a terrorist event. Whoever did this was likely a scientist, or scientists, probably working for a faction, possibly homegrown, perhaps a rogue. Maybe even someone they knew. Most were silent, just listening, stunned at events that had taken place. They worried about their families, and what all this meant, long term.

He listened to them and agreed that it was a tragic attack, with New York City targeted again. The impact of the attack was beyond comprehension. None could forget 9/11, and now this? One of the questions from the group was if any group or terrorist cell had taken responsibility. Dr. Adams advised them that he had no knowledge of that, but the FBI as well as other agencies were working to find whoever was responsible, and hopefully the perpetrator or perpetrators would be found quickly. He asked them to cooperate fully with the FBI.

Dr. Chen was listening from the back of the room. It took great effort for her to maintain her professional demeanor during this discussion, but she did.

Adams concluded the meeting, saying they would be asked to work overtime. They were to conduct themselves as normally as possible. All work done at the lab was considered classified, and they all had signed confidentiality agreements. Their work was not to be discussed outside of the premises. He would be making further announcements as information became available. After thanking them again, Dr. Adams concluded the meeting.

Suzy walked back to her office. She went in and closed the door, and tears started flowing. She put her head down on the desk, her beautiful hair falling around her shoulders, her sobs uncontrollable. How could I have done this? She knew why. She thought of the "Organization" and became frightened. Their threats to kill her sister were real and terrified her. Could she trust such a sinister group? Her parents would be boarding the flight momentarily to Hong Kong, where they were to pick up Lee. She would have to focus on them and nothing else, except Max. Suzy needed to call him. He must be concerned, hearing the news of the terrorist attack, and she needed to know what was going on with him. Did he suspect? How much did he know? She grabbed her phone to call him. He must be frantic, and Suzy needed to hear his voice.

He answered on the first ring.

"Max, I am sorry I haven't called. It has been so busy here. You have heard, of course."

"Yes, we are on alert, baby. How are you doing?" He had to be careful about his words.

"I'm scared, worried, and you know probably all that we know."

"Yes, we know what the so called 'weapon' is. It is having the desired effect. Disrupt and possibly kill.

"Yes," she whispered. "It can do that."

"I want to see you tonight. Is that possible?" he asked her.

"I don't know yet. Hold on, Max."

Stacy buzzed her. "Dr. Chen, you better come out. The FBI is here again. They are in Dr. Adams's office now. He wants you to report to him immediately."

Suzy got back on with Max. "I must go. The FBI is here. Guess they have to check everything out. This is horrible, isn't it?" she said.

"Yes. Call me when you can, and I will meet you at your place, okay?" he asked.

"Call before you leave. I don't know how long I will be here. Have to go, Max. I love you," hearing his "Love you, baby" as she hung up.

She knew he was concerned, but she couldn't be near him now. Too risky, and he would be questioning her. Not now.

# 53

eorgiana and Mark sat in front of Dr. Adams's desk. Lieutenant Randall, their escort, was waiting in the hallway outside Adams's office. George explained to Adams that they needed to do a thorough search, looking at computers, all records, and they wanted a complete inventory of the specimens stored at the Edgewood Labs, and most importantly, who had access to the stock.

Eric was waiting for Suzy to join them. "Where's the bitch?" he thought. She had talked to these two earlier, and he wanted her involved as much as possible. She could be the liaison with these clowns. They were wasting his time. He was confident that lab security had not been breached.

Georgiana said to Dr. Adams, "Our forensics investigative team is waiting outside. We must start right away." Then added, "We will do our best to make this quick and not interfere in the operations of this facility."

George could tell there was an undercurrent, maybe guilt or just Dr. Adams's egotistical disdain for authority. She didn't want to discuss their suspicions regarding Dr. Chen.

"Thank you, Agent Reed. Dr. Chen will be here momentarily. She will be more than happy to assist you," Eric responded, showing signs of impatience.

George could see this guy was used to getting what he wanted. What a pompous, self-centered A-hole. She gave Mark a look, and he responded with a quick eyebrow raise.

"Let me see if I can find her. Please excuse me." He walked out, heading toward Suzy's office.

George said to Mark, sick of waiting, "Screw him. Let's bring in the team."

George called Wally and asked if he and his group could please come into the building. Wally and his team had been in a white FBI van, in the parking lot, waiting for the "go" signal. The technical guys had the equipment needed to access information from the computer system and look at all video recordings. Wally would supervise the team and assist in the investigation.

Eric was still looking for Suzy. She wasn't in her office, so he went to Beth's office and barked, "Where the hell is Chen? Find her and tell her to show the FBI around the lab. It shouldn't take very long, and I am extremely busy." He wasn't going to deal with their crap.

"She went to the lab, Dr. Adams. She said she wanted to know the current status so she could direct the investigation properly," she said, without looking up.

Eric was sick of Beth and her attitude. He had taken her out for drinks a few times and she took it seriously. Now she acted like the hurt party. She seemed to enjoy the sex as much as he had. What the fuck. He would have to stop dating these office bitches. Adams stalked into his office, slamming the door. He had a headache and wasn't in the mood to deal with any of this shit.

Beth reached Dr. Chen and said that Dr. Adams wanted her to assist the FBI team in whatever way she could. The eight armed agents, including Wally, entered the reception area. Lt. Randall knew how to stay out of the way, but not miss anything. George, Mark, and Wally were discussing the strategy for the investigation when Chen joined them, surprised to see the large group waiting for her.

George spoke firmly, "We need to begin. Let's discuss what we need, and you can direct our team, all right?"

"Of course," she replied. "Where do you want to start?"

"The computer forensic science agents can do their thing, and other team members will need to examine the H5N1 inventory to see if it has been tampered with in any way. Perhaps you can give us some details and help show them around the storage facilities. Also, any updates on your latest findings would be most helpful."

"Certainly, by computers, do you mean our individual computers?" Suzy questioned.

"Yes," said George, "we need to check out all computers, lab stations, personal devices, smart phones, the whole deal. Let's start with Dr. Adams's computer, your assistant's, and yours also, Dr. Chen. Later, we will look at other staff computers."

"Follow me, please," responded Suzy without emotion.

# 54

Suzy had left George in her office with the tech guy as they began searching through computer data. They knew how to find legal forensic evidence in computers and digital storage media. Mark and Wally had stayed with the rest of the team, waiting for Dr. Chen to escort them to the lab. It wasn't a long wait. Dr. Adams had thrown a fit as another computer expert started on his laptop. "Tough shit," thought Chen as she joined Mark and the other team members in the reception area.

She led them down a long corridor through double doors, which could only be opened by a coded keypad. Two armed military guards stood on either side of the doors, and they acknowledged Dr. Chen as she passed through the entrance.

She explained to the group, as they were walking through the large laboratory, that the CDC was working in unison with the ERDC, looking at the recent findings confirming the diagnosis of the H5N1 virus on the recent admissions of not only the maintenance worker but others in various medical centers in New York City, Johns Hopkins in Baltimore, and a growing number of others. The CDC was tracking the pandemic, using recently developed software that gives a snapshot, state by state, of all reported cases.

"Our containment lab is in a separate part of this wing. I will take you there and show you our H5N1 samples, all intact. We have Level A airline protective suits for your safety. I have asked one of our lab technicians to print an inventory showing every 'bug' or toxin sample in storage."

Mark liked her clinical approach, but sensed she was holding something back. He hoped the investigation would expose what it was. He told her he needed the latest information and video on the delivery date of the H5N1 samples, including who received them.

"I received the samples, Agent Strickland," she said. "And I personally placed them in the secure containment storage locker."

"Show my men into the portal, suit them up, and let them check things out. I need to see the video of the delivery, and Hank, you stay with me, okay?" Mark requested of one of the team. Wally's handpicked agents knew exactly what they were looking for.

Mark said, "Wally, you want to stay here for the moment?"

"Fine with me," he said, looking around at the lab. It brought back some not so fond memories.

Mark turned his attention back to Chen and said, "Please show the guys how to safely access the storage unit so we can get this investigation moving."

"As you can see, we are very busy, Agent Strickland. Is all this scrutiny absolutely necessary?" Chen asked. "We are a government facility and wish to fully cooperate, but we have our orders also. We must work on a vaccine, and our security is beyond reproach."

"Your question is acknowledged. Now, let's get on with it. We need to see the delivery records, now," he emphasized. His patience was wearing thin.

She asked one of the lab assistants to show the FBI team into the safety portal.

Then Suzy said, "Follow me, gentlemen."

Suzy remained coolly detached. She took Mark and Hank to the delivery dock, explaining how specific items were received, when the deliveries took place, and then proceeded to the storage room where the records and videos were kept. Hank began unpacking his equipment to search the files and video recordings. He could handle this on his own. Mark wanted to see the rest of the facility, including the vaccine storage area, so Suzy led the way. They entered the lab and walked to the rear of the room where the cold storage for vaccines was located. She opened the door, allowing Mark to enter. She was looking at the various vaccines, labeled and arranged in perfect order, in vacuum-sealed containers. Suzy began explaining about the vaccine storage.

"We store most vaccines between 36 and 46 degrees Fahrenheit. They are to be used within a certain time frame, specifically during current influenza outbreaks. They have a very limited shelf life."

She stopped speaking, peering at one of the storage containers. The seal didn't appear to be secure. That was odd. She mentioned her concerns to Agent Strickland.

"I need to let Dr. Adams know about this immediately," and she asked Mark if he would join her in reporting this to Dr. Adams.

"Yes, and I better let my team know, also," said Mark, thinking George and Wally would be interested in this development.

# 55

As they were walking to Adams's office, Dr. Chen explained to Mark and Wally that the previous fall, she, Adams, and several others from the lab had attended an international scientific conference in Wilmington, Delaware. The topic of the conference was various methods of developing vaccines. Normally, vaccine manufacturing can take up to six months using the standard egg-based method, but six months is a lengthy turnaround when dealing with a pandemic. The new technique involved using various resources. They learned that the plant-based approach offers a substantially shortened production time and cost. If an outbreak is reported and the vaccine is available, the CDC can distribute it on the first day from the SNS, or Strategic National Stockpile. Plus, developing a specific vaccine and having it available for use quickly would greatly impact the response time to life-threatening bioterrorism threats and infectious diseases. This was a major breakthrough. Suzy and the others from Edgewood found it exciting, as did all those in the scientific community.

She didn't tell him what else had happened at the conference, which was held at the luxurious Tidewater Hotel and Conference Center. The meetings would start in the morning, giving the attendees plenty of free time in the afternoon, for recreation, committee meetings, or relaxation.

Suzy and Eric, as she called him then, had been seeing each other for several months. It was inappropriate for her to be dating her boss, and she knew the dangers. But he was intriguing, handsome, and their work interests gave them a common bond that added more depth to the relationship. This made the attraction even more interesting. Suzy had felt he was a perfect match for her, though he could be restrained and even distant at times. His elusiveness increased her desire. She tried hard to please and captivate him.

They had separate accommodations at the hotel, neither wanting their colleagues to know they were having an affair. But after hours, when they thought the others in their group wouldn't notice, Eric would slip down to her room on the third floor and find Suzy waiting for him, dressed in a provocative see-through baby doll nightie, or just a satiny silver bustier, panties, garter belt with spiked heels, or nothing at all. It didn't matter to Eric. Whatever she wore, or didn't wear, drove him insane and gave him an instant, throbbing hard on. Just thinking of her made him hard. They had uncontrollable sex, and she pleasured him in every way he wanted. They shared exotic tastes and loved sexual exploration. He never got enough of her hot little ass and tits. He was an aggressive, demanding lover, often ripping her clothes off, unable to wait.

She craved his attention and need for her and believed that he meant all of his declarations of love, for her alone. She had started dating him, not just because he was her boss, but for the intense attraction she felt. It was quite a compliment to know that a man of such merit and intellect would be interested in her. She honestly enjoyed the status but wasn't after anything beyond his love and the sexual excitement. She fulfilled every pleasure he demanded to win his love.

It wasn't until after she had been promoted to assistant director that she found out the truth. They had a Saturday evening dinner date, and he was to pick her up at 6:00 p.m. at her condominium. He was going to take her to their favorite restaurant, a small bistro that featured not only delicious cuisine but a wonderful pianist and singer. Suzy loved going there, and as regulars, they had gotten to know the singer, who always played their favorite song. It was a sappy love song, but it was beautiful and expressed lyrically how she felt about him. Eric had said he was tired, though, and needed the afternoon to catch up on his sleep from their previous all night sex romp. Suzy decided to surprise him and stopped by his house, wanting to sneak into his bedroom, crawl into bed with him, and wake him up in a delicious, intimate way. Although she had no reason to suspect, she wanted to make certain he was home alone, as he had said.

Eric always left the side door open into his kitchen. His red Corvette was parked in the driveway so she knew he was home, which erased any doubts of his faithfulness to her. As she walked into the kitchen, everything looked orderly, as usual. Soft afternoon light was coming through the window. She slipped off her heels and walked quietly to the bottom of the stairs. Placing her purse on the floor, Suzy took off her leather jacket, slacks, and rose-colored sweater and left them folded on the linen-covered chair in his foyer. Wearing only her pink demi-cup bra and matching sexy thong panties, she crept up the carpeted staircase. She was getting turned on thinking of him, eager to make love. She reached the landing and turned left, passing the guest bathroom to reach the master suite at the end of the hall. His bedroom door was closed, but as she approached, she heard voices. She froze in place and tried to hear what was being said. She recognized Eric's voice but not the other one, which was distinctly female.

Was this possible? The words weren't clear, but they were clear enough. She grasped the door handle, turned it slowly, opening the door and saw the unthinkable. Eric was in bed, his back to the door. He was clearly naked, and there were a woman's legs wrapped around his waist, and his movements made it obvious that he was fucking some whore, whoever she was.

He was so engrossed that he didn't even hear the door open until Suzy forcefully slammed it and ran down the stairs, not able to leave quickly enough. Eric managed to catch her as she was struggling to get her shoes on while racing for the kitchen door.

He had his slacks on, unzipped, barefoot, shirtless, and he was saying, "Suzy, please, Suzy, let me explain. Please." He was pleading with her, but she was crying and wouldn't look at him, as he tried to grab her. He kept saying, "This means nothing. Please understand. She stopped by and came on to me. I barely know her."

But Suzy heard nothing. She raced to her car, not even sure how she got in, and drove away, but that was the end. Without trust, there was nothing.

All of this was floating through her mind as she remembered the conference and how important it had been, not only the memories of the breathless love she had felt, which had shattered her heart, but the significance of the conference to her work. She had to quiet her random thoughts and her bubbling anger over the betrayal and her own stupidity for believing everything he had said. And it was only later that she realized, she had not been the only one he had betrayed.

# 56

uzy and Mark walked past Beth's desk. Beth was stressed by the events playing out around her. She hadn't been questioned yet, but knew she would be at some point. She and Eric had exchanged numerous intimate emails and she didn't want to lose her job, or worse, be implicated in whatever was going on around here.

Suzy knocked on Dr. Adams's office door and he said, "Come in," in a louder than normal voice. He was on his cell phone, but said an abrupt good-bye. He was obviously pissed off that this FBI geek was examining his computer.

Mark asked Ray, the FBI tech, "Got anything?"

Ray said, "We can discuss this later. Okay?"

Mark knew that meant something was up, and it had to be handled just right. Mark leaned down, over Ray's shoulder while Suzy was talking to Dr. Adams, explaining the possible problem, a compromise in the vaccine storage room.

Suzy was standing next to Eric by the bookcase, saying, "Dr. Adams, one vial of H5N1 is missing from the containment room. A decoy vial was found in its place. We've had a security breach."

"Oh my God." He was stunned. "You received those vials, right?"

"Yes. All the vials were there when I placed them in the containment room. They were stored securely," she stated.

Eric had no reason to doubt Suzy. She was a bitch but he was certain she was not involved.

"I need to check this out. Please come with me, Dr. Chen" Eric directed.

Things were hitting Dr. Adams from all directions. He was exhausted from the afternoon at the motel, which hadn't gone exactly as planned. It had been a cat and mouse experience with the bitch and ended in a wrestling match, but he finally got her convinced that she was the only one. She had flirted with him and agreed to the lunch date, but then played hard to get. Fuck that shit.

Now he had to deal with the subway debacle and this fucking H5N1 outbreak. Dr. Adams was a womanizer, but he was also qualified for his job, had worked hard, and was a highly regarded and brilliant scientist, above all, who took his work seriously. His dedication and competence were the only reasons Suzy had stayed at Edgewood, though her motivation had changed abruptly after the Organization contacted her.

Adams said to Mark, "I need to accompany Dr. Chen to the lab."

"Okay, I am going to stay with Ray." Mark added, "Please report back here, both of you, after you have looked into the vaccine matter. It might be significant in the investigation." He called one of the team to go with Chen and Adams to the lab.

Dr. Adams glared at Mark, not used to being told what to do by such a lowlife, and responded contemptuously,

"Certainly."

Adams and Suzy left, walking quickly to the lab and the cold storage room.

Mark called George on her cell phone, telling her that she might want to check out the vaccine storage room with Dr. Chen and Dr. Adams."

"Boy, I'm glad that asshole is out of my hair, for the moment, and I think I have found something," Ray said to Mark.

Ray knew his way around a hard drive.

Mark asked, "What is it?"

After Ray explained, Mark said, "I want this laptop sealed, and we will take it back to headquarters as evidence."

"I assume you got fingerprints," stated Mark.

Ray scowled at Mark, "You're kidding, right?"

"Let's get Chen's computer, and I think we need to start asking them some questions," added Mark.

"How about the assistant's laptop?" asked Ray.

"Yes, we will look at them all. Their phones, too."

# 57

The hospital beds were filled in the isolation unit at All Saints Hospital. Several of the staff members weren't feeling well. They were being tested for the virus, lab results pending. They were in the isolation unit.

Dr. Grant had been on the phone with Dr. Ambrose. Grant knew that they weren't the only facility dealing with the virus. The CDC tracked pandemics, and from their statistics, most hard hit would be the highly populated areas. It was too soon to gauge the spread of this outbreak.

Jim Lucas was making sure that the staff was being rotated with many resting in the lounges between shifts. The numerous disaster drills had paid off. Everyone was working at optimum level, and the professional atmosphere was beyond reproach. But there was an undercurrent of unexpressed fear.

Thank God people were heeding the Mayor's request for calm, so far. New Yorkers took most things in stride and were doing what was necessary to handle an unusual situation. Some were skeptics and felt invulnerable. They had survived

9/11 and refused to let out of the ordinary occurrences rattle them. There was the occasional patient that arrived in an anxious state but most remained calm. They were being kept for observation and were comfortable staying at the hospital, "in case." But to most New Yorkers, it was just another day in the Big Apple.

Lucas was following the news and had heard about the Century Air flight that was cancelled in Miami. It was the same plane that had two sick flight attendants, leaving one at Johns Hopkins in Baltimore and the other hospitalized in Miami. Apparently the captain had made the decision at the last minute to cancel the flight.

"What the hell," thought Jim, "This whole thing is getting out of hand."

He was worn out and prayed his hospital could get through this crisis. The practice drills and instructions were all well and good, but reality is never so simple. He had spoken with several other hospital administrators in Manhattan, and they were getting buried with new patients, some legitimately sick, others needing observation, many just frightened. If this was the beginning, where was it going to end?

His phone rang. "Yes, Dave. What is it?"

"I'm sick, Jim."

"Are you in your office?" Jim asked.

"Yes, I am going over to isolation. Frank knows. Call Vicki, please. I think she needs to know. Tell her to stay home with the girls. They are not to go out under any circumstances. Also, tell Chris. She is with a patient. Take care of her, Jim. She has been exposed, also. Keep her away from me—do you understand? You need to lock down the hospital. Take care, Jim."

"Yes, Dave." Jim heard Dave start coughing and the phone disconnect.

"Oh my God," he thought. "We are so fucked."

He was checking his contact list, looking for Dave's home number. As it was ringing, he felt the rush of cool air blowing on him, and he looked up at the vent directly above his desk. His stomach tightened in fear.

# 58

Mike Ryan was glad to hear the announcement that schools were closed as a precaution. Summer vacation was starting next week anyway. He wanted his boys at home, safe and sound, and Annie was available to babysit if he could get in to see Maggie tomorrow.

He was sick of listening to the repetitive news coverage and wasn't sure what to believe. He hoped this was an isolated event, but he was realistic. The Mayor underplayed it, but it was a big deal. As a scientist, he knew the dangers and possibilities, but tried not to go to the "what ifs." He would keep calm for his boys, and he would be there for them. He would do everything that Maggie would want him to do. He was praying hard and had faith that God would take care of his beautiful wife and their baby. They had talked about wanting another baby, hoping for a little girl. He was shocked but happy to learn that she was pregnant. His feelings were so mixed up. All he cared about was Maggie.

He wondered how Terry was doing. She was a good friend of Maggie's and the fact that she was in the hospital in Miami was more than troubling. "What does all this mean?" he wondered.

The news continued to be disturbing. More cases of the avian influenza virus were being reported, not just in New York City, but in Miami as well. He hoped and prayed this epidemic wasn't out of control, but he had sufficient reason to doubt. This bug was new and unpredictable. Its airborne characteristic made it even more dangerous. He hoped the CDC would find answers soon, but his main concern was for Maggie and the safety of their boys.

He was restless and eager to meet the boys after school and walk them home. They could stop by the deli and bring home sandwiches, potato salad, and snacks. He knew they would have plenty of questions, wanting to see their mom. He hoped he could keep his composure and be reassuring. Not just about Maggie, but about the subway attack. It scared the hell out of him. That would not be easy to hide. He would make sure Annie kept the boys inside. He checked the website about pandemics and found information about face masks and recommendations, including stocking up on supplies. He would stop at the market on the way home, also, and pick up some extra groceries. In case.

# 59

Georgiana followed Chen and Adams into the refrigerated vaccine storage room. A large storage container appeared to be improperly sealed. Dr. Adams explained that all the vaccine containers were marked with certain code numbers, which defined the vaccines. George and Suzy stood quietly by as Eric cross checked the code numbers.

He said, looking at the list, "This vaccine is not on the list. The container number is correct, but the number on each storage vial is different. These particular numbers don't appear to be anywhere on this list."

Suzy, apparently perplexed, responded, "Let's look at all the containers and see if we can get some sort of ID from them. Perhaps someone mistakenly marked these or moved a storage container."

Neither Suzy nor Eric believed that was possible. They were searching carefully through the large storage container, wearing sterile gloves, trying to find a label that would identify the mysterious vaccine. This room was used infrequently, only as vaccines were needed. Most were for rare contagious diseases, such as polio, smallpox, and others.

Adams looked frantically for some confirmation of the contents of this container. This one had no known origin or label, but someone in the lab must have knowledge of this. How could this mix up be accounted for? Eric had no idea and was perplexed that he had missed this.

Trying to remain calm, Adams said, "Indeed, this is quite remarkable."

He was looking deep inside the container, and then, on a boldly printed sticker, were the letters and numbers: **H5N1**. It was a large container, and in it were possibly innumerable doses of vaccine.

As the realization of what he may have found hit him, he turned to Dr. Chen and said, "What do you make of this?" He was clearly incredulous at the discovery.

Suzy reacted, "I have no idea," and she seemed shocked as well.

George said, "Let's check for fingerprints," though George knew that was highly unlikely.

The forensics scientists would have to check out exactly what was in the vials. They would get the CDC to help as well. George didn't want the Edgewood staff to be involved any further. Her bullshit meter was off scale.

George had been watching Chen and Adams very carefully, and her instincts were on high alert, big time. She wanted Dr. Ambrose here, or someone from the CDC, to oversee the work of his staff. The FBI needed to begin the interrogation process of the Edgewood department heads, specifically Chen and Adams, and others who might provide evidence as this situation was becoming more complex. She had ordered background checks on all those who worked at Edgewood and hoped something would stick out and give them a lead.

George stepped out of the room and called Ambrose on his cell phone.

"Yes, Agent Reed?" She explained the situation, and he said, "I'll arrange to send extra staff there immediately."

"The most experienced chemists from the CDC and FBI are needed to analyze the vials to determine if it is indeed the H5N1 vaccine," thought George. "How the hell did it get there, if it was actual H5N1 vaccine? Was it somehow connected to the perpetrator or perpetrators of the terror attack? How brilliant but also an anomaly. What kind of desperate insanity would result in such action? There were many twists in this bizarre event, but George was determined to figure them out. If this was vaccine, it must be determined quickly. How many lives might be saved?" Her thoughts were scattered.

George's cell phone rang. It was Jim Berger, one of the forensic techs who had been examining the stored vials of H5N1. He had stepped out of the viral storage room and removed his biohazard gear to place the call.

"Yes, Berger. What have you got?"

He responded, "We checked out the H5N1 vials, and after examination, we discovered one of the vials is empty."

George said, "Are you sure?"

He said, "Yep, and the Edgewood lab guy confirmed it. He was pretty upset to say the least. Guess he came to the same conclusion I did."

George said, "That the perp could be someone he works with and trusts, right?"

"Yep," he said.

"Great job, Berger. Can you bag the evidence safely?"

"Done," he responded.

"I want the room sealed and guarded. Got it?"

Yes, ma'am," he said, pleased with the discovery.

# 60

Suzy didn't get to her condo until after dark. It had been an exhausting day. The FBI interrogation was thorough. Suzy had been released, but they were still talking to Adams. Suzy had not requested an attorney, but Eric had called his immediately. He wasn't sure what was going on, but as head of the department, he knew that if anyone was going to be held responsible, he would be the target, no matter what evidence, if any, was found.

From the news reports she heard when driving home, Suzy knew that the virus was spreading. She had done everything the Organization had required of her, and she hoped they lived up to their agreement. They didn't know about the vaccine she had manufactured, and she hoped they wouldn't. The Organization had provided a large sum of cash for her mother and father, the roundtrip airplane tickets to Hong Kong, and all documents necessary to allow Lee to enter the United States. Suzy hoped she had covered her tracks well enough that nothing could be linked to her. The Organization had promised protection.

"Max will be here soon," Suzy thought.

All she had to hold on to was Max and the thoughts of her parents and Lee. Seeing him was dangerous, but she couldn't say no. She needed him and the comfort of his loving arms. If only for one last time. For his protection, she must tell him nothing, only that there is an investigation. Nothing more.

She touched the garage door opener and pulled in, parking her Lexus in its usual spot. She grabbed her purse and briefcase, opened the car door, and stepped out. The silent figure slipped into the garage, crept up to her car, two feet behind Suzy, and placed the muzzle of his BerettaTomcat .32 ACP, loaded with hot FMJ rounds, at the base of her skull and fired one crisp, clean shot into her brain stem. She fell instantly onto the concrete, her purse and briefcase scattering, her legs askew, one black high heel resting near her small stockinged foot.

The figure slipped out, undetected, hidden in the darkness behind her condo. He reached the street and began a light jog, looking casual, just another jogger out for his evening run, in black baggy running shorts and lightweight gray nylon jacket. The Tomcat was invisible in the palm of his hand. The passive surveillance tracking device he had placed on her Lexus several months ago had paid off. He smiled.

# 61

M egan Evans, the charge nurse, was checking Joey's IV. He was in the military hospital at Edgewood Medical in isolation and on a ventilator. He had pneumonia, high fever, and unstable vital signs. The anti-viral medications were so far ineffective. Though young and healthy, Joey had a high exposure volume of the toxic virus. His prognosis was bleak. Megan was worried, having never seen patients reach such a severe stage of infection so quickly.

Captain Sanders was the attending physician in charge of Joey's treatment as well as the other stricken members of the subway crew. They were all struggling with fevers and acute respiratory symptoms. Marty, Joey's boss, was extremely ill with pneumonia. Sanders had never seen or heard of such a virulent strain as this H5N1. Onset was sudden, and the duration of the infection was unpredictable. He had spoken to Dr. Ambrose from the CDC, but Ambrose had no definitive answers regarding duration or incubation period of this particular mutated strain of the avian flu virus.

Sanders walked into the isolation ward and spoke to the unit clerk, Barb. She smiled a hello, and he sat down next to her, looking at the computer screen, reading the patients' charts. His concerns were growing. Megan had recorded their recent vital signs, and they were unstable. Joey was worsening rapidly. The anti-viral medications had not helped, and Sanders was running out of treatment options.

Sanders walked over to Megan, and asked, "What do you think?

Megan responded, "It doesn't look good."

Sanders said, "Let's get the families on the phone. Damn, I hate making these calls."

Megan looked up and said, "Are you going to have them come here?"

She was worried about the contagion, even for herself, but she tried to hide her fears. She didn't feel the families should be near this facility, in spite of the imminent deaths of their loved ones.

"It will be their decision, but they need to know the status. Please ask Barb to get them on the phone. Joey's family first."

Megan knew, just from the obvious physical signs, that it wouldn't be long. Dr. Sanders was facing some tough phone calls, but the families were facing far worse.

Suddenly, a loud beeping noise came from the monitor next to Joey's bed.

Sanders said to Megan, "He's coding! Get the cart. Stat!"

Megan grabbed the cart, and she and the other nurse rushed to his bedside. Joey was in cardiac arrest.

They administered drugs into Joey's IV to stimulate his heart, and Sanders began CPR, but it was futile.

"Damn!" said Sanders under his breath.

# 62

Wally speculated, "Could be a shadow terrorist cell pulling all the strings."

Wally, George, and Mark were in one of the vans in the parking lot, discussing the interrogations. Dr. Adams was still being held inside the lab, but they had released Chen. She seemed to have little to contribute, and her laptop was clean. Adams denied any knowledge of the incriminating e-mail. He was nearly out of control with rage and indignation. Adams was asked to remain in his office, not charged, at least not yet.

Mark said to Wally, "Somehow, I don't think Adams is lying. That's my gut."

"But what about the e-mail draft on his laptop?" asked George. "*Mission accomplished. You will be wearing diamonds very soon, my love.*' That is concrete evidence in my book," she said.

Wally, sucking down another cup of stale coffee, said, "I hear you. Maybe a 'dead drop?'"

He paused, wondering who picked it up. Then Wally asked, "Mark, your take?"

They were all exhausted and felt they were close but missing something.

Mark said, "It is strong evidence, plus the H5N1 decoy. He could have done that or someone else inside. We can hold him, but I think someone with access could have gotten to his laptop and set him up. We need to find the person intended to pick it up, if anyone. It was 'dropped' today."

Wally said, "Inside, definitely. Whoever had access to his computer, but we need to take him into custody, right now. Everything points to him, period, and until we find other evidence, this bastard isn't leaving our sight."

"Hank found nothing unusual on the video showing Chen receive the H5N1 delivery and place it in storage," stated George. "At least nothing obvious. He is going to examine every video carefully from the night of the delivery to present."

"Something fucking happened, assuming all the vials were present and accounted for, as Chen said," said Wally.

"She had military escorts," said George, wondering how and when the exchange could have occurred.

Mark had been watching George, his eyes on her lips when she spoke. He wanted to kiss her, among other things. Damn. She still looked beautiful, after this exhausting day. Her long red hair, pantsuit, nothing out of place. Mark was distracted. He was going to take her to a late dinner when they could get away, even if only for an hour. He sensed something between them, and he often felt her looking at him. He couldn't stop thinking about her.

Wally and George were still trying to make sense of all of the evidence when George's cell phone rang.

She picked up the call. "Georgiana Reed here." She paused. "Oh shit, oh my God." She got out of the van and started pacing. "Did they get him? You are shitting me. Fuck!"

"I assume you are still looking for the shooter," she stated.

"Yes, go in and toss the place from cellar to attic. I think we might find some missing pieces. Thanks." George hung up.

Mark and Wally had stopped talking; both staring at George.

"Chen's dead. We had a tail on her, and after she pulled into her garage, she didn't go into her house, and our guys got suspicious when her car door remained ajar so they checked it out. They found Chen dead, one shot, back of the head. It looks like a professional hit. There were footprints near the garage entrance. The killer had a head start, but they are searching the area."

"Fucking A" said Wally.

All were still, and then Wally said, "A loose end, maybe."

# 63

George and Mark had gotten to the condo as fast as they could. Wally stayed at the lab with the task force. The day had been grueling, and they were tired and hungry. But they wanted to see everything firsthand. Chen's condominium was cordoned off with yellow tape and lots of flashing lights. Neighbors were standing in their driveways but couldn't get past the police barricades near Suzy's place.

"What have you found?" were the first words out of George's mouth when she spoke to Don Patterson, lead guy at the scene. He knew they were coming and was waiting at the curb when they pulled up in Mark's Mustang. Don was tall and slender, African American, all business. He explained what had been found. The manila envelope with the photos, the cryptic message, and Dr. Chen's personal laptop, bagged and ready to be taken to the FBI lab. Her S&W .38 J frame was also part of the evidence.

"Anything on the footprints?" Mark asked.

"Nope, not yet. Looks like a man's jogging shoes. He ran through the back, same way he came in." He gestured toward the right side of the garage. "We'll try to do a match, but the shoe is an average size and a common style," he answered. "No trace of him. The ground is dry, nothing on the pavement on the streets behind her place, but we found something more interesting downstairs."

George said, "Lead the way." She and Mark followed him inside, careful to not touch anything. George and Mark were looking around, admiring the beautiful décor. It was immaculate, as well. They could see the kitchen, very modern, and yet it appeared warm and frequently used. They took the stairs to the basement, following Don.

The "basement" was actually a carpeted game room, with casual, comfortable furniture, a flat screen TV on an antique console, end tables with tall burnished silver-based lamps, and several numbered prints, all large, modernistic of bright sweeping colors. A powder room with shower was in the far corner, near the small laundry room, which was hidden behind louvered doors. Nearby was what appeared to be a closet, with yellow tape across it. The "closet" was the jewel.

"Don, what's in the closet?" asked George. She assumed it housed the furnace and air-conditioning.

"It's a small but well-equipped laboratory. No one can enter until forensics checks it out. They are on their way. They will need to wear protective suits, in case," and he nodded his head.

George understood and said to Mark, "This may be one of the missing pieces."

Mark said nothing. He just kept looking around, trying to digest everything that had happened.

He said, "Clever girl."

"We assume you have some background on Chen," George stated.

"Yes, but not what you might think," he added. "The NCS has had her on their watch list for a little over a month. Nothing has occurred out of the ordinary. She has been involved with a certain Army Lieutenant Colonel Maxwell Graham, West Point grad, special service chief to the Joint Chiefs of Staff, a straight arrow. He reported some findings to a friend of his, a fellow West Point grad, Greg Hammond, who works for the NCS. Dr. Chen had full security clearance and excellent credentials. We had no reason to suspect her, and our surveillance has been steady but never came up with anything. Colonel Graham has been watching her, let's say, very closely." He raised his eyebrows. "They have been hot and heavy since January, this year."

He continued, "From the NCS investigation, we know that Chen also had previous involvement with Adams. It ended badly. She caught him with his pants down, banging some broad— excuse me, Agent Reed. I guess he paid Chen off with a promotion to assistant director of Edgewood Labs. There were two others in line for the position ahead of Dr. Chen, but she was proven capable and apparently had received several notable mentions in scientific journals for her work."

"This gets more and more interesting," George said.

"Here's another angle. Her mother, a native of China, Rose Lee Chen, met and eventually married an American chemistry professor. They met in Hong Kong. He was there on business, consulting for a major chemical manufacturer headquartered there. He brought his wife and her daughter, Suzy, back to the US. Her adoptive father is a professor at the University of Delaware, and her mother is a pianist, having taught piano in Beijing before being allowed to move to Hong Kong. Rose's first husband, Suzy's biological father, died in a labor camp in China when she was a baby.

"Rose's husband, Dr. Robert Thompson, adopted Suzy and loves her as his own. He is unaware that there is another child, a twin sister. Rose was only allowed to have one child under Chinese law. The Chinese authorities took her other daughter and placed her in a government orphanage. She is Suzy's identical twin. She only learned about her twin sister, Lee, this past year. Lee is living in Beijing, surviving as a prostitute. We don't know exactly how or when Suzy learned this."

"Interesting and puzzling," said George.

"There's more," said Don. "A Swiss bank account, ten million US seems to have some tie to Dr. Chen."

"Okay," George was impatient. "Whose name's on it?"

"No name. Just a number."

# 64

Lee didn't understand what Lou E was saying.

"Please explain," she pleaded.

"We must hurry, Lee, before the other girls awaken," was all he would say. Tears were flooding down her sculptured face, her eyes reddened and swollen from crying. He had knocked on her door very early and then entered her room, carrying a large black nylon suitcase. He placed it open, on the foot of her bed. He started filling it with her belongings from the rattan dresser drawers and her small closet.

She continued, "What have I done wrong?"

As she kept asking him what he was doing, he remained silent, and she sensed he was unhappy. She knew he cared deeply about her. She had been there now for more years than she could remember. It was the only life she had known. Lou E was much older, and he was like a father and husband to her. After he had gathered and packed all of her clothing, except for her personal items, he went over to Lee, who was sitting against the far wall of her bedroom, sobbing. She couldn't look at him. He sat down next to her and pulled her against him. His strong and loving arms were wrapped around his beautiful Lee, his love. She leaned into him, feeling loved and safe.

"Lee, my darling child, it is not my choice, but by government order. You must fly to Hong Kong immediately."

She held him tighter, more upset than ever by his words.

"Why?" She was trembling with fear. "Am I to be killed?"

She knew prostitution was illegal and thought that she was to be punished. Lou E and Mick had always protected their "charges" and paid large sums to local government officials for protection. The girls entertained them lavishly and felt honored to be with such notable and important guests.

"No." Lou E was reassuring, but solemn. "I have been told to place you on a flight this afternoon to arrive in Hong Kong by this evening. Someone will be awaiting your arrival at the gate, and you will be safe and well cared for. You are to have no fears or concerns."

He would not tell her that he and Mick were paid a large sum of money to arrange her transfer. They also had no choice. Mick and Lou E were heartbroken. Both felt great love for Lee, having known her from childhood to womanhood. She had a beautiful spirit and felt great affection and love for both of these men. Lou E had become her exclusive lover, and he allowed no one else to touch her. As Lee's role shifted, she befriended the new girls and helped them adjust to their new world. She felt fortunate to have been cared for by such devoted men. They were her family. It was the only life she had known.

Lou E stood, pulling her up with him, held her, kissed her forehead gently, and said, "Shower and prepare yourself. I have bought some travelling clothes for you. You will be pleased with the new garments, shoes, and other items that I have chosen."

She trusted him to do what was best for her. She always did his bidding. She looked up at him, into his loving eyes, and gently kissed his mouth. They felt the love between them that was everlasting. She went into the bathroom, removed her silk dressing gown, and when fully undressed, stepped into the warm shower. As she washed her hair, and felt the water flowing over her soft skin, she suddenly felt an excitement and trust, that there could be a new world, something wondrous in her future. She had read about Hong Kong, and the idea of going there was like a dream. The unknown was still frightening, but Lou E had always protected her, and she knew he always would.

# 65

Max called Greg at his DC office.

"Greg, I need to talk to you," asked Max.

"Of course," said Greg, and he paused.

"Is it true that the NYC subway was attacked by terrorists this morning?" asked Max.

"Yes," answered Greg.

"What are you allowed to tell me?" Max asked.

"The FBI is working the case, and they are starting at the logical place," he answered.

"Edgewood," stated Max in a monotone.

"Yep," answered Greg.

"So there could be a link to the director and others who work there?"

"Anything is possible," answered Greg.

"Cut the crap. You know what I need to know." Max was pissed.

"Dr. Adams and his staff are being questioned. Forensics is there now. Some items have been taken for further examination," answered Greg. "Remember Wally Weber, the FBI guy from the anthrax case?"

"Yes, I recognize his name," said Max.

"He is a big gun behind the scenes, and I heard through the grapevine that he is part of the investigation team," stated Greg.

"Shit," said Max. "I need to talk to Suzy. She cannot be involved in this. She and the director dated for a short time, but something happened and she ended it," stated Max. Max sounded like he was trying to convince himself.

"He is being interrogated. He is denying any knowledge or having any information that could link him to the H5N1 outbreak, though evidence is pointing directly to him. They think he had an accomplice. At least preliminary evidence indicates that, but we don't know who, as yet," said Greg.

Greg had to ask Max, "Do you think she is still involved with Adams?"

"Fuck no, no way," answered Max, angry that Greg had even gone there. "Motive?"

"Adams had an expensive divorce, so he could use some money, or he could have a hard-on for the US or he could be a fruit fucking cake," said Greg. "Maybe all three," he added.

"Evidence?" asked Max.

"E-mails," said Greg. Then he continued, "From Adams to a dead drop, indicating a completed task, and other incriminating stuff. Of course, he denies any knowledge of this."

"Maybe a set up?" asked Max. He prayed to God that Suzy wasn't part of this shit. He had to see her right away.

Max was tired of waiting for Suzy to call. She wasn't answering her cell phone, and he knew she was no longer at the lab.

"Shit," Max exclaimed. "I guess that's all you can say, right?"

"Right, except stay away from her for now. Do you understand?"

Greg was being forceful and cared about his longtime friend, but he knew Max would not listen.

"I'm on the way to her place," said Max, ending the call.

"No!" yelled Greg, but Max had already hung up.

# 66

Max was driving as fast as he could, sensing something was seriously wrong. He hoped that Suzy wasn't involved. His mind couldn't conceive of that possibility. He would know when he saw her, held her, and she would tell him everything. All he had to do was look in her eyes. He knew of Suzy's desperate need to save her twin sister, Lee. Knowing what he had learned from Greg about her sister and other emotional entanglements, he understood more fully how tortured and damaged Suzy's life had been.

The drive seemed to take forever, but he finally made it to the Bayside Retreat entrance. Normally he would just key in the security code, and the gate would rise. Instead, he was being questioned by a Maryland State Trooper asking for his identification.

"What the fuck," he thought as he pulled out his military ID.

"Good evening, sir. What is your business here, Colonel?" asked the state trooper.

"I am here to visit a friend, officer. What's going on?" asked Max.

He is alarm bells were going off, big time, and he was getting impatient, as well.

"I am not free to say. What is your business here, sir?" the officer repeated.

Max tried to relax and smiled, "My girl, she lives just a few blocks down from here, 62 Sandpiper."

The officer studied Max, his high-ranking Army uniform, and said, "One moment, Colonel."

The trooper pulled out his radio and spoke for a few moments. "Yes, ma'am," was all Max heard.

"You may proceed," and he raised the gate, knowing what was ahead for this guy.

# 67

Max couldn't get near Suzy's condo. He parked as close as possible and then ran to the edge of the cordoned off area. He was stopped by a muscular guy, dressed in a dark suit, wearing an earpiece, and obviously carrying.

"What's going on? My girlfriend lives in this building," Max said loudly, and was struggling with the big guy, trying to see over the flashing lights and people, many in uniform, some on cell phones. Suzy's condo was brightly lit, and he could see the open garage door.

"My name is Agent Walker, FBI. What is your name, sir?" asked the big guy.

"Colonel Max Graham."

"Some ID, please," requested the agent.

He was inspecting the military ID while Max continued to look at the activity near the building.

"Hold on, Colonel. Let me contact the agents in charge of this investigation."

Max backed down, hands on his hips, impatient to understand what was happening.

"What's taking so long?" he thought.

"Sir, Agents Reed and Strickland would like to talk with you. Just follow me," he requested.

Max followed closely behind Walker, heading toward the condominium.

"Thanks, Walker," said George.

They introduced themselves to Max. "I'm FBI Special Agent Reed and this is my partner, Agent Strickland." They shook hands.

Max said, in a commanding voice, "What's happening here? I would like to see Dr. Chen, Agent Reed."

She responded, "Let's go to the police van. It's a bit more private, and we can talk," she directed.

Max followed her, stepping into the white unit. Mark remained silent but accompanied them into the van.

George said, "Let's sit down here at the table. "

There was a small built-in table with bench seats on either side to the right of the door. Max sat on one side, and George and Mark slid into the seat opposite him.

"Colonel Graham, please tell me about your relationship with Dr. Chen," she asked.

Max was glancing around, noticing others working at computer monitors, but he couldn't quite stay focused. He felt confused and uncertain of what was going on.

"Look, I will tell you all I know, but I need to see Dr. Chen and know that she is all right. I have been trying to talk to her for most of the day and could only speak with her briefly. I understand about the investigation and the need for security, but she and I are," and he hesitated, "involved, on a very personal basis. Do you understand?" he asked, intensely. "Tell me what's going on. Now!"

George touched his arm gently and said, "Colonel Graham, Dr. Chen has been shot by an unknown assailant and is dead."

# 68

Annie had bathed the boys, dressed them in their jammies, and then they curled up on the sofa in the TV room, watching a video. It had been fun having the sandwiches and potato chips although they missed their mom. But Annie was nice, and they loved being with her.

It was around 9:00 p.m. when Mike began the drive to Baltimore. He wanted to get to Maggie as soon as possible. He couldn't wait any longer. He had called the evening shift nurse, saying he was coming, and asked about Maggie's status. The nurse, Jeff, said she was holding her own, but her prognosis was uncertain. He told Mike that he would be able to look at Maggie through a glass partition and talk to her through an intercom but that was all. Mike didn't care. He had to be with his wife.

Dwight, from crew dispatch, had called earlier that evening, totally distraught. But somehow, he managed to get the words out. Terry had died that evening, and Mike had broken down. How could this nightmare be happening?

His eyes were still puffy from crying, but Mike focused on the drive. It had been easy to find the hospital. He parked near the emergency entrance, where one of the clerks directed him to ICU. Maggie was in an isolation unit on the same floor. After thanking the clerk, Mike hurried down the hall.

He got to the unit and was directed to a waiting room, where there were several others sitting quietly, hoping for those few moments when they could see their loved ones. A TV set was on in the corner of the room. The news reporter was talking about the growing fears of a dangerous pandemic.

Finally, after about thirty minutes, Jeff called for Mike and led him to a small private room with a large glass window. Mike listened as Jeff explained which bed Maggie was in. All Mike could see was a large clear canopy around her bed, and tubes and monitors everywhere. But he could see a blurred image of her face, looking as though she was in a deep sleep, her body very still. There was a phone on a table beside the window.

Jeff said, "I'll go in and place the phone next to Maggie's ear, and you can talk to her. Dial zero-six and we will be connected. It'll take me a few minutes to get my mask and hood on."

Mike nodded. "Okay." A few minutes later, he saw Jeff enter the unit and go into the canopy. Mike dialed the number.

Jeff picked up and said, "Go ahead." Then he placed the phone near Maggie's ear.

Mike began talking to her, very softly, saying, "Maggie, it's Mike, I love you, sweetheart. Don't worry. The boys send hugs and kisses. You will be home soon. I am going to spoil you. And the boys will love their new brother or sister, our baby, Maggie."

He just kept talking to her, telling her everything she needed to hear.

Jeff turned around and spoke into the phone, "Her eyes are open, Mike. Your girl is a fighter."

Then Jeff hurried off to report to the doctor and get further instructions. Mike had tears running down his face, as he stood, head bowed in quiet prayer.

# 69

ater that evening, Mark and George were driving to their Baltimore hotel, talking about the case, needing to decompress from the trying day. They had much work ahead, putting together the various pieces of this still unfolding crisis. The presumed vials of the H5N1 vaccine were at the CDC, and the Edgewood Facility was under heavy guard. Much of the evidence continued to implicate Adams and Chen. Chen's murder further complicated the investigation. It had been difficult telling Max about Suzy. The man had maintained self-control but was clearly devastated. George realized at that moment that no one is promised tomorrow.

Mark appeared deep in thought and then asked, "How about a late dinner?"

Hesitating, Georgiana looked up from her notes at Mark. He was staring at the road ahead, hands gripping the steering wheel, waiting for her answer.

"I have wanted you to ask me that for a long time," she said, reaching over and touching his hand.

He brought her hand to his mouth and kissed her palm tenderly.

# EPILOGUE

He smiled to himself. How well things were going. The deadly pandemic and the resulting panic had been achieved. Many had died, and more deaths would follow. He delighted in watching the American economy go into free fall, giving him great advantage, knowing his holdings would grab investments at the low and gain huge profits. The American recession would last many years, and what was once a super power would be no longer.

Damn. Too bad Suzy had to be disposed of. She had fit so perfectly into his scheme. She would have been a great sexual toy aside from being ornamental. He enjoyed games so much. But she was bright and had done her job well, and she did get what she wanted. He had managed to arrange with his Chinese "friends" to release her sexy little twin sister. Wasn't that enough? And he had to protect himself and those who were loyal employees, so to speak. It had been easy to find mercenaries, as well. He chuckled out loud and walked to the large window of his office, overlooking the Thames. There were still some loose ends, but his Organization was well equipped to deal with them at the proper time.

As a respected international industrialist, he could move many pawns around without suspicion. The money took well-planned circuitous routes and never could any links to him be found. His support of the jihadist group was untraceable. They needed him. They got what they wanted, to destroy the filthy, stupid American pigs, and he would continue to amass a fortune from the failing American economy. Greed was the motive, but the chase was the pleasure.

He glanced at his Breitling, realizing he must hurry. He had a luncheon appointment with the Chinese ambassador. He must not be rude to someone who had done him such a great favor. They were meeting at the Chinese embassy, and he looked forward to many of the specialty Chinese dishes, especially the delicious pork and rice, spring rolls, and dumplings. He had epicurean tastes in all things. He was certain there would be some beautiful Chinese women there, eager for his attention. Exotic desserts were always the finishing touch to a gourmet meal, providing the most delicious of all pleasures.

# ABOUT THE AUTHOR

Raised in the south, Linda Wells attended the University of South Florida and went on to become a flight attendant for a major airline. *Dead Love*, her debut novel, fits into her favorite genre of mystery thrillers. Wells and her husband live in Columbus, Ohio, and she is currently working on her new novel.

Made in the USA
Lexington, KY
06 April 2019